WAKING UP EIGHTY

Be Careful What You Wish For

Shola Lawrence

Contents

Waking Up Eighty

INTRODUCTION

Swift feet pass by frozen blades of green grass.
Few and far between they are, unlike the usual swirling mass.
Early in the morning, her thoughts turn to the past.
The pain of being left alone lies there,
And the waves that her hair makes as she swims in the depths
send ripples all around her…

"Kara!"

The loud call disrupted the amateur poet's concentration. She took one last look at the page before ripping it out of the notepad and balling it up into a decidedly rough paper sphere, tossed it in an arc towards her trashcan.

She missed, of course.

She left the discarded poem to the floor with a sigh of surrender and dragged herself out of bed. Her mother had likely as not already woken every man, woman, and child that had the good fortune of still being asleep at 6:45 on this cold winter morning.

Most mornings were like this. Kara would wake up, and her mind would go racing through time and space, seeking out the one thought that was sure to sour her mood…

Dad.

One treacherous tear began to form at the edge of her vision, and as quick as lightning, Kara flicked off the moisture and blinked. She knew the score. That one drop would lead to a trickle, and pretty soon, she would be seated on the ground, bawling her eyes out.

Not today, thank you very much.

Her dreams had started it all, as usual. She'd been flung into the past, reliving the day she understood that her dad had abandoned her. Kara had dreams like this all the time, and they were far too vivid for her liking. It was almost like going back in time for real.

As these thoughts drifted through her mind, Kara had flung herself under the shower and attacked her mouth with her electric toothbrush. She was deep in her thoughts and halfway through putting on socks when the sound of her name came through the window once more.

"Kara! What's taking so long?"

This brought her back to reality. How long had her mother been waiting outside?

I meant to keep her waiting, but not for this long. Jeez.

Throwing on the rest of her outfit and grabbing her jacket off the rack, Kara ran down the stairs and out the front door…

CHAPTER 1

Act Out

The snow fell gently onto the hood of the old Honda, as the rickety engine continued its low, stuttering drone, breaking the still morning air. Sitting in the driver's seat of the once black car, Emma ran a finger through her once black hair. Likewise, it had once also been black. Now both were going grey and getting more so by the second as she sat waiting for what seemed like hours for her daughter.

"Kara!" she screamed for what felt like the hundredth time. "What's taking so long?"

She cringed as her voice rang out in the early morning atmosphere. The neighbors were surely sitting up in their beds and judging her by now. Emma sighed, checking her makeup one more time. It was precisely the same as it had been five minutes ago.

Just as she braced herself to embarrass herself some more, the front door swung open. Kara, her often frustrating daughter, hurried out, nearly tripping at the stairs' base.

"What took you so long? I swear, I spend more gas waiting for you than it costs to get me past the free-way…"

Kara ignored the complaints, sliding wordlessly into the passenger seat and tossing her backpack behind her. She used just to toss it through the window, but one miss had left a particularly nasty dent on the car, as well as a cracked calculator screen.

Even rebels learned from their mistakes once in a while, after all.

The wheels crunched the snow as they made the slow maneuver out of the neighborhood and onto the larger roads leading into town. The two drove on in the same odd silence for about three minutes, until it began to irk the older woman.

"Why do you always do this to me, Kara? I really don't understand it."

Kara had been expecting this. She averted her eyes, choosing to gaze out the window and ignore the bait. She'd had this conversation before. More often than she cared to.

"It's getting old, y'know," her mother continued, un-fazed by the silence. "Sooner or later, I'm gonna need you to be more responsible and not…"

"I **am** responsible." Kara's response came out be-fore she could stop herself. It always did. She rolled her eyes as the usual sarcastic laughter rumbled low in her mom's throat.

"Responsible? Is that what you call that mess at Sarah's place over the weekend? Responsible behavior?"

"Do we really have to get into this now, mom? Really?" Kara retorted, scoffing and turning her head just enough to put her mother in her peripheral vision.

"Oh, we're not getting into it right now, young lady. But we will. As soon as you get back from school, your father and I are going to…"

"Father? You mean Dale? Dale's not my dad. But I just can't wait to get back and listen to him pretend to be."

The sarcasm in her tone was much more glaring than the voice that delivered it. Emma exhaled sharply and thought for a minute before asking a question.

"Why do you hate him, Kara?"

That got a reaction. Kara turned and gave her mom an almost quizzical look. This wasn't usually part of the program in these spats.

"He's trying really hard, y'know. He works, he listens, takes care of us. He makes me very happy."

Emma pulled over, bringing the car to a stop beside a hydrant with a small poster advertising magic sets. Kara looked longingly at it, wishing she could vanish. Her mother looked her dead on and continued.

"So why do you keep doing things to upset him? Why do you act like you want him mad at you?"

Kara's lip turned up. She had been fazed by the original question. But now they were back in familiar territory. Accusations.

"I've never done anything to him. He just doesn't mind his business."

"That's not true. You've done tons of things to get on Dale's nerves. Some of them required a baffling amount of effort to boot. The only thing you haven't done is give him a chance. You refuse to let us be a family like we should be."

Kara looked away, weary of the conversation.

"Can you just take me to school and save the lecture for later?"

Emma opened her mouth to say something but thought better of it. She shook her head sadly as the car began to move forward once more, the silence just as heavy as when the ride began.

*****

Truman High was one of the oldest buildings in the world. Or at least, it looked that way to Kara. As her mom pulled up to the curb in front of it, she felt her heart fall. It always did when they got here.

I don't know which sucks more; this place or living with Dale and mom.

Reaching behind her for her backpack, Kara pushed the door open, frowning at the sound the old door made as it swung out. She was already halfway out of the car when she heard her mother beckon to her from the driver's seat.

"Have a nice day, sweetie. I love you."

This gave her pause, but only for a fraction of a second. She wasn't about to let her mom guilt her into regretting her actions.

"Kara?"

Kara shut the door then, making no answer to her mother's call. She felt a twinge of the guilt she was fleeing, and it only got worse when she heard the sad sigh from behind her before the car moved on.

Why does she always have to do this crap?

Even as the anger welled up, tears followed suit, blurring her vision slightly. Kara switched to a brisk walk, making a beeline for the nearest bathroom.

If there was one advantage to the horrid early wake-up call, it was the lack of company at times like this. As she made her way to the restrooms, only a few other people flittered about. They were mainly maintenance staff and student government types with early meetings. No one that she cared about.

After washing her face twice with the ice-cold tap water, Kara stared into the mirror for what seemed like an eternity. The treacherous tears were gone, but her mood was already irreparably spoiled. She sighed, grabbed a paper towel, and dried her face.

No one cares about your blues, Kara. Chin up. You have a ton of homework to do.

She hurried off to find a quiet corner to work in, finally regretting her weekend excesses.

But not really.

*****

Hours later, Kara was still in the exact same funk. It was the period before lunch, and her mind was everywhere except the stuffy classroom that her body was in. She was just about to retry her cringy little poem from earlier when something broke through the fuzz.

"Kara? Would you like to tell us the answer?"

Her name took her by surprise and scattered her thoughts to the four winds.

That needs to stop happening. Jeez

"We're waiting, Kara."

The algebra teacher, whose name she couldn't be assed to remember, was staring at her through glasses as thick as a club dancer all the way from the board. A quick glance told her all she needed to know to confirm that she couldn't answer the question; it was algebra.

"I can honestly say I have no idea what any of that is. Algebra just isn't my thing, sir."

For a moment, Kara thought she had just dug herself a hole. The sincerity of her words might have been a bit too much for the situation. And it certainly looked like the man was going to tell her off.

"You and every other student, it seems," he said with a sigh. "Pay attention, class. I'll only go through this once..."

Breathing a sigh of relief, Kara's mind returned to its higher plane of thought and stayed up in the clouds until the bell dismissed the class.

Kara gathered up her things and headed out the door, meeting up with her friend Sarah, who had been waiting at the door for her.

"Hey, Kara."

"Hey. Enjoy algebra?"

"Well, I like math," Sarah said, as they began to make their way towards the cafeteria. "but Mr. Green's class is always so boring, y'know? I barely learn anything at all. You spoke for everyone in there, believe me."

How did I forget the name Green?

Just as Kara said something about falling asleep faster than she could spell Green, the two girls came up to a group of jocks hanging around the double doors to the gym. As they approached, one of them, a tall, handsome brunette breaks off in their direction.

"Hey, George! Saw the game on Saturday. That was a great pass. Thirty yards with no effort. Epic."

The happy, soft-voiced girl standing in front of George had not existed moments prior. Sarah looked on in amazement as her newly transformed friend exchanged pleasantries and sports stats with George until he excused himself to head down to the field.

"What was that?"

Kara looked at Sarah with the sly grin she always had on after one of these spats.

"I have no idea what you're talking about, Sarah."

Sarah gestured to the line and proceeded towards it as she spoke.

"You sure? Because unless I was at the mall grabbing a smoothie with your long-lost twin sister, you were about as far away from the game as you could get under the same area code."

"So, I told a little white lie. Big deal."

"Yea, but how did you even know that?"

"Oh, I asked Luke to go and fill me in on what happened."

"Luke? That one weird friend of yours that comes in early to study the pool water?"

Kara scoffed as they exited the line.

"He's not my friend. He's just useful every once in a while. And he doesn't come in every morning. God knows I could've used the help with my homework this morning.'

As they settled into their seats with their trays of inedible mashed potatoes and fruit, Sarah continued her interrogation.

"Why do we do that?"

"Who?"

"Girls. We drop these subtle, nuanced hints that we're interested, fully knowing how clueless guys are. Why don't we ever just take the direct approach?"

Kara laughed; her mood had vastly improved from just an hour prior.

"So, like just walk up to him and go; Hey George. I think you're a hunk, and I wanna make out with you and have your kids. That'll end well."

"Seriously??"

"No," Kara said, prodding the 'food' with a fork. " I'm not that forward. I was exaggerating, but you get my point."

"Okay, well yeah. Why wouldn't it? What's the worst that could happen? Think he'll run off screaming?"

Kara thought about it for a second and said, "Yeah. Maybe."

The two girls laughed, and Kara tossed a sauce packet at Sarah in faux anger.

"Better my subtle approach than your hide and seek game with Pete on Saturday. That was crazy, even for you."

Sarah blushed a bit at this. She was tall and pretty, with clean blonde hair and green eyes that sparkled in the sun and really good at math. But for some reason, she still totally lost her mind around Pete.

"Well, that's true," she retorted. "But at least I didn't take a few shots and total my dad's car so..."

"Dad? You mean Dale? He's NOT my dad, okay?"

Sarah immediately regretted her word choice, seeing Kara's mood shift back.

"Sorry. Stepdad, then. How screwed are you?"

Kara huffed a bit, her George-induced high successfully crashed.

"Take a guess."

"He exploded?"

"Not yet. The Kara Is Canceled party happens to-night when he gets back from work."

"Do they know about the drinking? Because my dad would kill me if he found out."

"Nah. I think we're safe on that front."

Sarah breathed a sigh of relief and started on her homemade sandwiches. At the same time, Kara looked at her mushy, greenish potatoes with weird longing as her stomach rumbled.

Just as Sarah reached over to offer Kara a sandwich, a girl walked over to them with her lunch tray. She had dark skin, and pretty black hair braided down her back. It was clear to the girls that she wasn't in their grade.

Just great. A junior.

"Hey! I'm Gelisa. Would you guys mind if I-"

"Get lost, loser. This table's taken."

"Oh," the new girl said, clearly hurt. "Sorry to both-er you."

As she slunk away with her head down, Sarah gave Kara a look that clearly said, what the hell was that?

"What?" She said, biting into the sandwich. "It is."

*****

Hours later, Kara lay in bed, flipping through the pages of a reader's digest she picked up last week.

She had some music playing over the radio set to low, and she was starting to feel a bit better.

Dropping the magazine, she stared loosely at the hot pink wall and furniture, her thoughts drifting steadily, unfocused.

I wonder how long this peace and quiet is gonna last?

Before she could even make a guess, the answer came storming into her room in a white shirt and work shoes.

"Family meeting. Downstairs. NOW."

Dale was a big man with a loud, booming voice. So, when he walked into a room and spoke in a stern tone, Kara was pretty sure he was impossible to completely ignore. She certainly couldn't, even after preparing to do just that all afternoon.

He turned on his heels, heading back to the living room, where the annoying lecture was going to occur.

Well, isn't that great?

Kara got up, shutting off the music and heading down. She tried to shut her door behind her, but it hit her wooden doorstop instead. The sound of it brought a judge's gavel to mind.

Fitting, considering what's about to happen.

As she finished her descent, Kara walked into the living room to see her mother seated on the sofa facing the entranceway, with Dale standing beside her. He looked livid, so he had probably just heard the news. Kara shot her mother a venomous glance before settling into the chair opposite.

After a few seconds that felt more like minutes, Dale took a seat next to Kara's mom and looked at her.

"Kara, tell us. What did you do this weekend?"

"I was at Sarah's." The answer came almost immediately." I went over on Friday after you left for the convention, we hung out, and I was back by Sunday morning."

"Are you sure you're not missing out on any details? Do anything fun, maybe?"

"Do anything fun, maybe?" Kara mimicked, mocking his deep voice. "No. Nothing out of the ordinary."

The straight face he'd had on till then vanished very quickly at that. It contorted slightly with what was definitely a look of extreme annoyance.

"Don't play games with us, young lady. We know you took the car out on a joyride and wrecked it. AND we know about the drinking."

That took her by surprise, and it showed. She'd never hoped to believe that Dale was dumb enough to not notice a missing headlight and messed up bumper. But the other thing...

"Yea, that's right," he said, seeing the shock in her eyes. "Sarah's mom told us everything.

"Well, Sarah's fucked then," Kara said, remembering the other girl's assertion that she'd be killed.

"Watch your language, young lady!" her mother yelled, furious. "What is wrong with you?"

"Fine. Fine. Can we just skip to the part where you punish me, Dale?"

That ticked him off a notch higher. He started to say something, but then calmed himself. There was some more silence, in which he took her mother's hand in his.

"Why do you do this, Kara? You're a smart kid. You know how this ends up. It's like you're trying to get yourself punished."

"Well, maybe I do."

"Of course. Always a witty reply, huh? You know what I think? I think you need a hobby. Maybe more than one. Then you wouldn't be so idle all the time, looking for fires to start. Maybe a part-time job would-"

"A job? I'm sixteen. You can't make me work. There are child labor laws."

"First off, that's not what that means. I've been working since I was 13, and it's been good for me. Secondly, no one is forcing you to do anything. It's a suggestion. I was always busy, and I never got in trouble with my parents."

"Y'know, I can believe that. You should probably learn to live a little before it's too late, Dale."

That pissed him off, but he held off any more steam, then asked in a much calmer voice than she expected,

"Why are you so disrespectful? Why do you do things that make your mom feel like you're antagonizing her on purpose?"

That one hurt, but Kara just rolled her eyes, intent on keeping this as short as possible.

"How are we supposed to trust you when you can't even be left alone for two days without acting out?"

That does it. I'm sick of this.

"You know what, Dale? Maybe that's something you should figure out. Because I sure as hell don't have an answer for you."

Before Dale could respond with his newfound restraint, Emma shot out of her seat, eyes burning like coals in a furnace.

"Kara Elizabeth Stewart. You will show your stepfather some respect, or so help me-"

A hand on her shoulder stopped her in her tracks. But that was a green light for Kara. Unlike Dale's weird therapist attitude, anger was an emotion she was used to.

"Yes, mother."

The mockery in her voice was more scathing than she'd intended. Her mother's face shifted from rage to what seemed like confusion. And then, slowly, she began to sob.

Kara was alarmed and made a motion to go to her, but Dale was already there. He wrapped his arms around her, whispering in her ear till she calmed down. And then, he looked at Kara over her shoulder, and suddenly the calm was gone.

"You see what you've done? Are you happy now? You'll keep hurting her like this on purpose. Is that what she deserves?"

"It's what she gets till she stops trying to force you into our lives."

Kara knew she was being very unreasonable. Even as she said the words, she was swamped with regret more profound than she could process. But she stood her ground.

"Well, you wanted punishment? You got it. You're grounded for three months. No friends coming over, no sleepovers, no allowance. And no phone, too."

"Wait, what? You can't do that!"

"I can, and I have. If you don't appreciate the things we do for you, then we can start doing a whole lot less."

"I'm not giving you my phone."

"That's fine. You can just pay off the rest of the contract on your mobile, buy your own minutes, and get your own Wi-Fi."

"You can't do that!" she yelled, turning to her mother. "He can't do that! It was a gift from you."

"It was a gift from both of us, and Dale's been paying for all of it. And it was my idea to take it. So, go ahead and yell at me some more."

All the guilt that had been orbiting Kara's heart suddenly rushed in as her mom spoke. The loud, angry voice was broken, choked up by tears, and what Kara thought might have been regret. She could no longer look either of them in the eye, and when Dale stretched out a hand, she retrieved her phone from her back pocket and handed it over with no further fuss.

"Since you won't have a phone or an allowance, one of us will swing by from work to pick you up every day. Early. It'll be during our lunch break, so don't expect any time to socialize."

"You've gotten what you want, so just leave me alone."

With that, Kara stormed up the stairs to her room, leaving the two adults in silence for a short while.

"I swear, she used to be such a good girl. Where did I go wrong?"

Dale hugged his wife tighter and shook his head.

"It's not your fault, honey. Kids are like that. She'll mature soon enough. I promise."

*****

Upstairs in her room, Kara lay in bed, staring at the ceiling with empty, red eyes. At first, she'd raged, pacing around her room and throwing things. But the irrational anger had quickly given way to sadness. She'd cried till her eyes hurt, and her nose ran. Then she collapsed on her bed, feeling empty and hopeless. Sleep came for her, but wouldn't remain. She passed in and out of consciousness, with just one thought permeating both states.

I hate them. I hate them. I hate them.

The tears threatened a return, but she was too exhausted to fight them anymore.

"I can't wait to grow up and move out of this place."

She'd been thinking that for years, but saying it out loud, on that day, made her realize that she didn't need to wait to escape.

She sprang up from her bed, walking silently to her room's door and listening with her ear to the wood panel. She could hear the muffled speech from her mother's room. The walls were so thick, there was a good chance they wouldn't hear her walk past. She knew this from years of progressively louder music blaring from her stereo.

Moving away from the door, she hastily packed a bag with what she thought would be the bare essentials. All the while, she silently cursed Sarah for convincing her to spend all her allowance on booze. Not that she really regretted it. The point had been to piss off Dale.

And oh boy, did it work.

By the time she was done packing, Kara had fully come to her senses and realized that she couldn't actually run away from home. She wouldn't last a month, and that felt like a pretty generous time limit.

But that didn't mean there was nothing to gain from staying away from them. At least for a week or two. Maybe the not so subtle reminder that she could leave would get them to give Kara some breathing room. Maybe her mom would even finally let go of Dale.

A girl could dream, right?

Kara snuck past the other bedroom, her backpack in one hand and her shoes in the other. She got past the landing and slid down the stairwell on the banister. She liked her chances better sliding than trying to go down the creaky stairs stealthily. Although it did seem somewhat goofy considering how serious the occasion was.

Once Kara was downstairs, the stealth came to an end, as she could shut the thick kitchen door behind her. Down here, outside lights didn't permeate the interior as much, so it was down to memory to get Kara around.

She stopped to steal some snacks from the pantry and toss them in a large fanny pack and fill up a water bottle. She planned to crash at her art teacher's house for a week. She was cool, and her mom loathed her hippie attitude enough to not have her home address or number. Seemed like a good enough call.

Well, let's see how well you get through a few days without me here to kick around, eh?

The front door was locked from the inside, and Kara knew she'd have to leave it unlatched. But then the neighborhood was safe. Nothing ever really happened here, so they'd be fine till Dale got up at 4:30. She closed the door as carefully as he could, pulling it up and toward the hinges to avoid creaks.

I have way too much experience with this type of thing. Maybe I do act out a bit too much. Not like that changes anything, anyway.

It was already morning, from the looks of it. Kara took a deep breath, internally recalling the path to Claire's place. Even now, it still felt weird calling a teacher just Claire. But she insisted. She was weird that way.

The night air was cold against her face as she stepped out onto the top of the short staircase, and there wasn't a soul in sight.

Which was just what I needed.

Any witnesses might try to stop her, after all. And it wouldn't be much of a runaway trick if she only got as far as the last building on the block.

The streetlights were on, each casting a perfectly circular pool of illumination onto the cool asphalt below. As Kara stepped onto the sidewalk, the low crunch of her feet seemed much louder than she'd expected.

That might be a problem.

Kara briefly considered going back for the keys to Dale's car. He'd apparently found time to have it fixed and cleaned up after work, and the thought of invalidating that appealed greatly to her. But starting a car engine in the middle of the night on a quiet street would be stupid, even for her.

She put her earphones in and picked her most recent playlist. It was the one she'd made over the weekend at Sarah's. As the first strains of restrained drums started, she continued down the street, sticking to the dark patches between lights.

*****

Two hours and several city blocks later, Kara was rethinking her runaway plans. She'd made only moderate progress walking along, and her shirt was already stained many shades darker with sweat. Her bag straps chaffed her shoulders, and her feet hurt a lot.

She'd expected all of that, though not as soon. What she hadn't accounted for was all the homeless people and late-night drivers that plied the same roadways she was taking. One particularly scary looking man had made her take a detour that had probably cost her a half hour on its own.

Keep it together, Kara. What sort of runaway is scared of a few old guys in the streets at night? Jeez.

Despite her best efforts, the lack of sleep began to take its toll on Kara. She hardly ever stayed up late, and when she did, it usually meant a very late morning for her. Needless to say, her body wasn't holding up well. She absentmindedly marched on, barely able to keep herself upright.

Screech!

Somewhere far off, the wheels of a car were laboring to hold against the cold, unforgiving road. Kara paid it no mind, as she was too tired to bother. What time was it? She was too sleepy to check. But she needed to know how late it-

Beep! Beep!

The same car sounded its horn, warning some poor idiot to clear off. The sound irritated Kara. Why did it need to be so loud? People were asleep!

More importantly, some of us are trying to pull off an escape.

The sound pissed her off so much that she decided she would take time out to go see what was happening, after all. But as she turned around to check it out, Kara realized something was wrong immediately. Her eyes flooded with light, blinding her and causing her to instinctively try to shield her eyes.

That was a mistake.

Already struggling to stand upright, Kara's balance was thrown off completely, and she tumbled off the thin sidewalk and into the road. As she fell, losing her grip on her bag in the process, her mind returned to full alertness and her predicament became clear.

In her drowsy state, her sense of perception had failed her and she had mistaken a very real and nearby threat to her safety for some far-off exercise in traffic etiquette. And now she was off balance, the ground rushing to meet her.

And the out of control car was doing the same.

Time seemed to slow, but Kara could no more save herself than she could fly. Her mind was racing with regrets.

CHAPTER 2

Rude Awakening

"Ahhhhh!"

The weak scream escaped from Kara's mouth involuntarily, leaving her perplexed. Her throat felt rattled and raw, and her vision was blurry, unfocused. This just adding to her confusion.

Where am I?

As her mind began to rise above the fog, Kara realized she was in a bed. The soft, threaded surface beneath her head said as much. The rest of the bed wasn't as comfortable, though. Her body felt weak and sluggish. She blinked a few times, and when her vision cleared, she found herself staring at a shockingly white roof above her. The room was dimly lit, though she could see no clear light source above her.

This isn't my bed or my room. Where am I? And why do I feel like roadkill?

A small stab of pain at the back of her head seemed to jog her memory.

I was... running away. So tired. Tires screeching and that damned horn giving me a headache... bright lights and-

All of a sudden, Kara's mind fixed in on the missing detail.

The car! I got hit by a car!

Immediately her system flooded with panic as she flashed through the last moments before the impact. But was there ever really an impact? She was clearly alive even though she felt terrible. Maybe the driver had managed to stop in time. Kara had heard about people losing consciousness due to fear or shock before, so it wasn't like there was no chance right?

I probably just passed out from the fear and got hurt falling. Mum and Dale are gonna be so pissed.

This calmed her down a bit but Kara was still left with the question of where exactly she was. This didn't look anything like the school Infirmary or the town Hospital. She had been to both several times and couldn't remember ever seeing such a strange white ceiling or lights that weren't above her head. Had she walked further than she thought? Was she in a different town? Kara vaguely remembered being about halfway through town on her way to the teacher's house. There was no reason she would be taken out of town for treatment.

By now, she had gotten herself together and decided to sit up to better get her bearings. But as soon as she did, pain shot through her back and she let out a low moan. She dropped back down on the mattress, using her right elbow to support her weight instead. But even that felt weak and fragile.

How did I manage to fuck up every last bit of me? I feel like a naked skeleton that fell down a hill.

From her half-raised position, Kara threw off the thick blanket with considerable effort. She could now see more of the room. It was small, with little other than the bed she lay on in it. There were no apparent light sources on the walls either, and they were just as shockingly white as the ceiling, as was the tiled floor. A thin line of black paint ringed the room and separated the walls from the ceiling and floor, as well as each other. There was also a mirror on the other end of the room, and a small bedside table close at hand, but the most pressing thing Kara noticed was the absolutely horrid nightgown she was dressed in. It was pink, with red roses sewn into it at the hem. The last time Kara had seen something that foul was at a school trip to the old folk's home. The curtains had been similarly decorated, and she'd hated it almost as much as she'd hated the smell.

Luckily, this room doesn't smell like old people. Come to think of it, this place doesn't smell like a hospital either.

Kara took a deep breath, hurting her chest a little in the process. There was no aroma present that she could detect. There wasn't any trace of the sanitized floor smell she was used to. It just smelt...

Empty. Like that time I lost my sense of smell because of my meds. Weird.

The undue sniffing gave Kara an itchy nose, and she sneezed a bit because of it, causing her hair to fall to her face. She usually wore it in a bun, but apparently whoever had dressed her had left it loose. Kara sighed and made to brush the erring section away. Loose wasn't her best look.

But as she brushed her hair away, she noticed a gleam of color that gave her pause. With a little trouble, she brought the mop of hair back in front of her eyes, and horror grabbed her by the heartstrings.

Her hair had gone grey.

She could tell it was actually grey, and not a dye almost immediately.

Did it go grey from the trauma? Isn't that something that only happens in movies?

Just as she was coming to terms with this and absentmindedly touching the hair, her eyes fell on her hand.

But it wasn't hers.

The digits and palm that held the stands of her now grey hair were wrinkled, with colored fingernails and faint blood vessels showing through.

What the fu-

The apprehension and dread that had taken hold of her gave way to panic, and she threw off the blankets and leapt from the bed, wincing in pain as she did but ignoring it. Her mind fixated on one thing and one thing alone.

The mirror. I have to get to the mirror.

She walked as quickly as she could, each step dogged by all round pain. But her mind numbed her to it as she made her way to the mirror. In moments she was standing in front of it.

But was she really?

The person staring back at Kara from the silvered surface couldn't be her.

Kara Stewart had clear, olive skin and long, luscious auburn hair. She looked about the same as most other 16-year-old girls in other respects.

But this mirror image was nowhere near 16. It had skin like an Egyptian mummy's and brittle white hair that hung out like straw all over, save for the front.

She looked 90 years old.

Kara stared into the mirror in disbelief. But suddenly, she could see it. She could recognize herself in the mirror. It was the same face, the same emerald eyes. Her little birthmark was there as well. And the figure did everything that she did.

There was no mistake. This was her.

And so, Kara screamed.

*****

Jacqueline Caro loved her job. About as much as anyone could, at least. Being a caretaker for the elderly had its ups and downs, like most other jobs.

But whether it was a good day or a bad day, one thing was constant; it was the most boring place on earth. Nothing ever happened at a nice little nursing home, after all. And while it sounded like a problem on paper, Jacqui was still undecided on the whole thing. But as she reclined in the staff idle area, she couldn't help but feel that the advantages to peace and quiet outweighed the need for anything exciting to happen, and the pay was decent.

And then, she heard the scream.

In a fraction of a second, Jacqui was up and running. Her instincts kicked in before she could even understand what was happening. Before she'd come to this nice and quiet place, she'd put in a few years at the Emergency Ward down at Central. And that training was still intact.

As she tore down the hallways at full speed, her mind caught up with her body. The scream had come from the Tranquility ward. This was strange as only the most quiet and unproblematic charges were put there, hence the name. If someone there was making a ruckus, then something very worrying must have happened. But none of the safeguards in the room had deployed and no alarms had sounded.

As she passed the second wing, she was joined by Barbara, another caretaker. She was the one who was in charge of monitoring Tranquility, and seemed just as worried.

"Any idea what happened, Barb?" Jacqui asked between breaths. Neither slowed down.

"No. We don't use video feeds to monitor Tranquility because we've never had to. But the noise sensor went off in room 16. Mrs. Kara Evans. She-"

Short of breath, Barbara cut her sentence short and came to a halt. A quick glance at the door labels told Jacqui that they had arrived at the right room. As Barbara unlocked the door with her ID scan and authorization key, Jacqui readied her mind for something truly disturbing. After all, preparing for the worst was part of the job.

The door slid open with a gentle hiss, and the air conditioning poured out into the hallway, cold rolling through both women as they quietly entered the room.

The lights were on dim, but they could see well enough to immediately spot the lady. She was standing in front of her mirror, a look that was equal parts horror and disbelief on her face. A quick glance around assured them that everything else was in place. As Jacqui approached the elderly lady, Barbara used the motion sensor control to open the window panel and increase the temperature a little. Jacqui reached out a hand to the lady, slow and steady. She was just about to tap her on the shoulder when Barbara increased the light level in the room, causing them all to blink as the ambient lighting flooded the room.

Apparently, the elderly Mrs. Evans hadn't noticed them prior to that. But now, she looked around and saw them, her face switched from the mask of despair to one of distrust, possibly anger.

"Mrs. Evans?" Jacqui said, trying to sound as reassuring as she could.

No answer. Still she looked on, her body language hostile. If anything, a look of confusion swept across her face.

"Kara?"

"You- You know my name. Did you do this to me?"

Jacqui had been expecting a more worrying situation. At the very least, she'd thought there would be some injury. But it seemed to only be a bit of elderly confusion.

"It's okay, Kara. We're here now. What's the matter? What happened to you? Is it something wrong with the controls or-"

Jacqui was stopped short by a sudden slap to the wrist from the elderly woman. She'd attempted to pat her on the shoulder, as a comforting gesture. But seemingly it was unwelcome. The woman had hit her, likely as hard as her old bones could manage, and then tried to distance herself. As she did, her back hit the wall, and she placed a palm on it, putting her other hand in front of her.

"Stay away from me." she said, in a shaky voice. "Who are you?"

"I-"

Jacqui was interrupted by a pat on the shoulder. Barbara stepped past her with her MedicDroid in hand, booting up.

"Mrs. Evans? It's me, Barbara. I brought you your meds when you had a headache a few days ago. Remember me?"

"Meds? What the fuck are you talking about? And my name's not Evans. It's Stewart."

There was a lot more worry in her voice now. Jacqui shot Barbara a quizzical look, worried that the charge might hurt herself. Barbara put a finger up and mouthed the word panic attack. She pushed a button on her MedicDroid, reading the information it displayed before answering.

"No, Mrs. Evans. Stewart is your maiden name." As she said this, she tried to approach her, letting the MedicDroid free. "You changed it when you got married. You're just having a bit of a-"

"STAY AWAY!"

It was clear that she was having a breakdown of sorts, and the strain she was putting on herself wasn't going to be good for her.

Barbara sighed, pointing to her elderly ward and snapping her finger. Immediately, the Droid Shot forward, spraying Mrs. Evans with a measured dose of a harmless but quick acting sedative. The droplets fell gently onto her arm, and in a moment, she was drowsy. As her eyes closed and her limbs relaxed, Barbara strode forward and held her gently, waiting for the sedative to take full effect. The old lady was a fighter, and she clearly didn't want the sedative to take effect. But eventually she succumbed and her weakened flailing ended.

"Times like this, I'm really glad Tranquil mist spray exists. Imagine having to go at her with the old syringe?"

"I get what you mean," Jacqui responded. "I still don't know how medical staff managed it without injuring someone."

She joined Barbara, taking the lady's legs and helping to carry her to the bed. There was a stretcher built into the wall for this exact purpose, but the caretakers found that it saved a lot of time to just do it the old-fashioned way when possible.

This one wasn't so heavy. If it was Mr. Jarvis though…

They got her to the bed with little difficulty, and Barbara set a reminder so she could come back when the sedative wore off. They returned the lights to the dim setting and exited the room.

"Jeez. I'm supposed to take over this section tomorrow. Does she do that often?"

Jacqui sounded a bit worried. She hadn't thought the duty rotation would come with any extra drama.

"No," Barbara reassured her. "I've never seen her or anyone else in Tranquility act that way. It's probably nothing. She probably just had a lapse in memory, then panicked. I'll inform the counsellors."

"So, what's her story?"

"Oh, same as the rest of 'em, really. She's old and can't take care of herself. Her family is either all gone or abandoned her to her fate. Lots of the usual age-related aches and pains, mild emphysema. She'd usually not so bad. Not that she's very nice either, mind."

"Ah. Well, I have a few months to get to know her. I'll probably learn the rest over time."

"Well, you'll have a lot of time to read up and speak to everyone. If you thought Kinetic was boring, wait till you've done a week of tranquil."

They both laughed at this, and said their goodbyes as they reached a parting of ways at the main reception. But as she walked away, Jacqueline found herself hoping that Tranquility lived up to its name, and that Mrs. Evans was okay. The internal debate about whether the boredom was a plus or negative had been decidedly settled. The little episode had brough back her feelings from the emergency ward with ferocious clarity.

When the subject was fragile human lives, peace and boredom were always preferable.

As an afterthought, she touched the button on the side of her MediGage. Her personal MedicDroid popped up from the gauntlet style holder, ready to receive instruction.

"Connect to Room 16, Tranquility Wing. Monitor state of consciousness, and sync noise and frantic activity sensors."

There was a beep, and a quick bioscan. Barbara's Droid had to confirm her identity to grant access to the monitors. She wouldn't have proper clearance for that wing until tomorrow, when she officially took charge.

Settling in her room, she wondered about Barbara's conclusion that the Evans woman was run of the mill.

There's something off about her. I'll have to wait and find out myself, I guess. At least there's the transition week to ease me into it.

She forced herself to clear her head, and slid into her bed space. Her thoughts drifted as she fell asleep, slowly settling on memories of her honeymoon…

CHAPTER 3

Sunnyside Up

Kara slowly came to hours later, her head feeling cloudy and unsettled. This didn't last long however, and the memory of her previous shock and the ensuing outburst came rushing back. Not that it felt real. There were a few details that made no sense. She thought she remembered being attacked by a floating robot.

Looking around, she was pleasantly surprised to see that the room she was in was different from the one she remembered. There was a window, with actual sunlight coming in through it, and it didn't feel unnaturally cold like she'd felt before. There was even a monitor on her bedside table.

This is more hi-fi than sci-fi. Must've all been a dream… Wait! If it was all a dream, then that means-

She got up once more with quite some effort, and walked over slowly to the mirror.

Whatever that crazy robot spray was, it really knocked me the fuck out. It's making me move even slower than I feel.

She reached the mirror, hoping against hope that she'd been hallucinating. After all, she clearly remembered the car accident. It felt more real than everything that had happened since.

But there was no such luck. She was still the same old person that she had been the last time she looked into the mirror. And now that she was calm and in daylight, it was obvious that this was no dream.

I've aged a million years overnight.

The weight of it all hit her then, and she returned to the bed, tears streaming down her wrinkled face. After a few minutes, she calmed down.

Okay, Kara. Think. No one can age that much in a night, even if they did get into an accident. And it's not a coma. I'd be brain dead or something, right?

She thought back to what she could remember from her last conscious experience.

Different name… Married, she said. And the sci-fi tech stuff…

And then it dawned on her.

I didn't age up in a day. I'm in the future. MY future. I'm Kara Evans now. Evans… That's George's family name! But he was older than me by a mile. If I'm here alone, and this old… he's probably already dead.

Everyone's *probably already dead.*

The thought did little to raise her spirits. This was her new reality, it seemed. At least, for however many years the frail old vessel she found herself in had left.

Was she going to die here, her whole life skipped ahead like a boring prerecorded soap opera episode?

Well, may as well find out the specifics. Starting with where the hell I am.

Kara approached the window, deciding it was the best place to start. She seemed to recall the room not having one before, but they had probably moved her to a more secure room after her little outburst. She'd have to remember to pretend like she knew who she was, even if she didn't remember. Old people forgot stuff, after all. Maybe they'd fill her in.

Peering out through impossibly thin glass that was cleaner than her mom's criminal record, Kara saw what was quite frankly more of a fairytale garden than anything even resembling real. Outside her room's confines stretched a picturesque meadow, with grass that looked almost dangerously green and red flowers so vivid they couldn't possibly be real. A few trees grew amongst the finery, thin shoots with white bark and ripe fruit.

This entire thing looks like a dream. But it's not. Meaning this… It's real.

Kara found her spirits lifted just from the view. The despair she'd been holding down vanished, if only to give her a brief respite. And then her stomach rumbled, and her tranquility was ruined.

On that high note, I think it's time I left this place. I'm starving.

The first problem, of course, was that Kara had no idea where the door was. She was reasonably sure that she wasn't being held prisoner, but that didn't mean whoever was in charge wouldn't restrain her after that incident. But she figured she'd try anyway.

A quick look around didn't help. The wall seemed to be perfectly smooth. But judging from the way the bed was positioned, the window and mirror's position, and where the two women had approached from, Kara made an educated guess and walked towards the left half of her room's west wall.

After half a minute or so, Kara started to notice something. A door sized portion of the wall seemed to glow when she got near it. It was hard to tell, seeing as her vision wasn't all that it used to be, but when she pressed her fingers to it, she could definitely feel something. A slight vibration, absent on other parts of the same wall.

That's either a door or- that's a door.

She pushed against the section gently, glad no one was there to see her look stupid if this didn't work. And for a moment, it didn't. The section didn't move an inch, even as she increased the pressure. But after a moment, it slid sideways into the adjacent section, revealing a large doorway. Poking her head out of the opening, Kara saw that it led into a hallway with an aesthetic similar to her room's interior. The walls all looked like they were made of the same strange white material, and the corners and edges were highlighted.

If nothing else, it's a pretty place. Now, how do I find-

"Good morning, Mrs. Evans."

"Argh!"

Kara spun around, her heart racing from the surprise. It hurt, and she clutched at her chest, leaning against the smooth, cool wall to support herself.

"I'm sorry, ma'am. I didn't mean to startle you. Feeling better now?"

Fuck no! I'm old and weak and in the future!

Kara had a million and one reasons to answer in the negative. But she'd already come to the conclusion that she was stuck here for better or worse.

If I really am stuck here, it would be best not to get myself thrown into the looney bin. If the future even has those.

"Yea," Kara responded, nodding slowly. "I feel much better."

"That's great. I can see it, too. We didn't get a proper introduction yesterday," the lady said. 'I'm Jacqueline. Jacqueline Caro. But you can call me nurse Jacqui. Or just Jacqui."

"Well, you already know my name. A whole lot better than I do, in fact."

Jacqui laughed a bit at this.

"It was just a lapse in recollection. Happens to everyone your age. We'll help you get things back in order. Anyway, I'm taking over from Nurse Barbara as a Caretaker for your ward. So, I'll be in charge of making sure you're okay. If you need any help or information, I'm your gal."

*Ah. She's the help. I might enjoy **this** a bit, at least.*

"Okay, Jacqui. First question, what year is it?"

"Well, that's an easy one. It's 2076."

Trippy. I lost 64 years of my life in a single night.

The thought threatened to send her back into her prior state of despair. But she blinked, held back a tear, and pulled through.

"So, I'm 80 years old, then?" Kara concluded after some quick mental math.

"Yes. As of a few months ago. You had a little cake and ice cream, remember? The geriatric kind?"

"Ah, right. I remember," Kara said, recalling nothing at all.

"By the way, we should get you to the dining area. It's breakfast time. You know the timetable here, right?"

As she said this, she put one hand on Kara's shoulder and gently led her down the hall to the left.

"Um, yeah. Totally." Kara responded, following along, the thought of food raising her spirits a bit. "Where exactly is here, again?"

Jacqui smiled. She'd expected this. As soon as Mrs. Evans had gotten up from bed, she'd been notified. She'd watched her fail to remember where the door was, as well. She was clearly not all there.

But there was something about how she spoke like a much younger person that made her think it might be more than just memory deterioration due to age. Protocol dictated taking her to a counselor, but somehow Jacqui knew that would be a bad idea. She decided instead to make it a pet project to help her.

After all, if Tranquility was as uneventful as she was told, she'd need a hobby.

"Well, this is Sunnyside Elderly Living Community. You've been here for about 2 years."

"2 years… And my family? Husband? Kids? Is my mother still alive?"

"Your mother has… passed. As has your husband. Right before you enrolled here, in fact. I think that's why you came to us. As for your kid… it's my understanding that your relationship with her was strained, at best."

Something about that sounds about right.

"But you must have some friends *here*, right?"

"I don't think so. At least, not that I remember."

Jacqui pursed her lips ever so slightly and continued moving.

Friends.

Kara's mind flashed to Sarah. She'd give anything to have her here. But that would be too good to be true. She thought of Annalise, Gemma, and the rest of her friend group. Could any of them be here?

The entire time the two women had been moving, their surroundings had been mostly uniform. On one side, the vast expanse of the white wall, with almost invisible indents, indicated doors and room numbers beside them. On the other, there was the same wall paneling. But here, it was broken by windows that looked out into more of the dreamy meadow that Kara had seen from her room.

Now, however, the corridor came to an end. They arrived at a large opening leading into a spacious little room with tables and chairs arranged artfully around the place, and a food counter at the far end. The furniture looked very sci-fi, with thin supports and lots of simple curves. They were just as white as the walls and the floors, but with red cushions that looked rather comfy.

About half of the spaces were taken up by other residents, all quietly eating by themselves. Jacqui steered Kara into one of the unoccupied ones, then waved over at a lady standing at the counter.

"I'm gonna go check on some other things now, okay? Roberta over there will see to it that you're well taken care of. If you need me, just call, okay?"

"Call on what? Hey-!"

But Jacqui was already off down the hallway where she came from earlier. Kara sighed, turning back to her table. The lady from the counter was walking over with a tray in hand. She was big and tall, with a stern expression.

Not the friendliest looking person here, eh?

As she approached, Kara's stomach began to rumble in anticipation.

"Hello. I'm Roberta. Will that be milk or water?"

The lady had reached her table and dropped the tray in front of Kara. On it, there was a bowl half full of a weird semiliquid with a spoon in it, and what looked suspiciously like one of the small, round tablets of soap you'd get at a hotel.

"Milk, please."

As the lady marched away, Kara turned her attention back to the tray. It looked extremely unappealing to her.

But hey, it's the future. Maybe it's not so bad, right?

Somewhere in the back of her head, Kara knew that was her stomach talking, but she couldn't help it. She gingerly picked up the spoon and tried a mouthful of the weird, odorless goop.

Bleh.

It was about as tasteless as it looked and smelled, with a texture like chalk in her mouth. She tried another spoonful and gagged at it, barely managing to swallow it.

The large woman known as Roberta came back with a cup of milk covered with a thin aluminum piece. Kara pushed the tray towards her as she approached the table.

"Hey. Roberta, right? Can I get something else to eat?"

"No, you may not. This is best for you. Now eat."

She had a voice worthy of her large frame, and her assertion drew the eyes of the room onto them. The elderly residents looked up from their various meals and activities, likely waiting to see how this played out.

"Did real food go extinct sometime in the last 60 years? I mean, we're paying to be here, right? We should get to eat things that taste better than *this*," Kara said, gesturing to the bowl.

At this, a few people muttered what seemed to be agreement. One or two people nodded.

"Well," Roberta said, giving her a stern look. "If you're so passionate about it, then don't have your supplement mix. We'll see how that plays out, eh?"

With that, she marched back to her station, the others avoiding her gaze as she went.

Kara felt like she'd struck a chord there, but it didn't change the fact that she was absolutely ravenous. She eyed the soap-like disc on her tray, picking it up and examining it. She sniffed it apprehensively and was delightfully surprised. It had the telltale scent of a pastry. She bit into it, still expecting to be disappointed, but she was not. It tasted as good as it smelled.

Delicious!

She scuffed it down in two bites, as quickly as her old bones would let her. It had a pleasant, strong aftertaste, and Kara was so hungry that she used it as cover to force down about half the bowl of slop. Fortunately, it was filling, and she was sated before the lingering sweetness deserted her.

As she turned her attention to the sweetened milk in the cup, a young girl strolled in. Kara's eyes followed her as she made her way through the room. She had long, blond hair with green eyes shrouded in heavy makeup, and wore jeans and a pink belly shirt. There were futuristic shades on her eyes with a clear glass front.

"Ellie!"

The young girl had apparently been sighted by the person she came to visit. An elderly man with a bald head got out of his chair, arms wide open for a hug. But Ellie sidestepped him and took a seat at the table he'd been sitting on.

Well, damn.

"Hey, gramps."

The man looked disappointed, but he quickly recovered and took a seat.

"How are you, sweetie?"

"Fine."

She barely seemed to care that he was speaking to her, staring blankly at him through her thin lens.

"Where's Tina?"

"Mom's at the office. She'll be here in a bit. I'm supposed to keep you company."

"Oh, that's-"

Before he could finish his response, Ellie touched the side of her goggles, and the lens blacked out. She began to gesture with her finger in the air.

"That was… thoughtful of her. How's school coming along?"

"Same as always," she responded, not breaking her trance. "It sucks."

"I see. What's that you're doing with your finger and the glasses?"

"Mobile game. Furious Feathers."

"Oh. Anything like Angry birds?"

"What's that?"

"Oh, it's a mobile game from when I was your-"

"Sounds dumb, grandpa."

The old man sighs, looking away from his granddaughter. As he did, he caught Kara staring and gave her a weak smile. She smiled back as best she could.

Maybe I should say something?

Just as she was about to go over and espouse her love for Angry Birds, the man's attention turned back to the entrance, and his face lit up. Following his eyes, Kara saw a lady that was clearly Ellie's mother walk in. She had the same nose and eyes and hair. Unlike her daughter, however, she was happy to see the old man and hugged him before his arms were even fully outstretched.

Kara smiled at the sight and decided she'd watched them long enough. She tried to get up, but her aging body wasn't built for such rapid movement. She'd half fallen back into her chair when a robust set of arms stopped her from behind.

"Careful there, Mrs. E."

Kara turned back to see the second nurse from the other night.

"Barbara?"

"Yes. So, you do remember? I'd certainly hope so, after 2 years of taking care of you."

As she spoke, Barbara helped Kara up to her feet.

"There you go. Take it easy, Mrs. Evans. You really should call Jacqui along when you need something. And you obviously haven't been taking your full dose of supplement mix."

Kara followed Barbara's eyes to the half-full bowl of slop.

No wonder it tastes so bad. It's literally medicine.

"If you don't eat up, you'll have to go back to taking the supplements in pill form."

"I'd prefer that, honestly."

"Really? Okay then. I'll have you switched to a regular breakfast then."

"Well, I better be going now. I have a whole other wing to see to. Remember, just call Jacqui if you need anything."

"How do I do that?"

"Just out loud. The monitoring system will notify her."

"Oh. Okay, then. Bye."

With a wave, Barbara went off to her new assignment.

*****

A week later, Kara lay awake in bed, unable to get to sleep. Over the last few days, she'd acquainted herself with the basics of living at Sunnyside. She had learned the room controls, the locations of the reception, cafeteria, the rec room, and a few other essential things, like how to open up the built-in bathroom. She'd learned that one the hard way, as well as discovering that her bladder really didn't hold up to pressure like it used to.

But what kept her up now was her thoughts. Memories swirled around in her head, torturing her. It didn't help that her body ached as well. The pills she'd been prescribed helped reduce the pains, but her memory wasn't at its best, and she'd forgotten to take them. But she couldn't tell anyone that. Kara gathered that if you needed special attention, you'd be transferred to another wing. She hadn't gotten the feeling that this was a good thing. So, she kept her forgetfulness to herself.

If I can't sleep, I may as well go pick up the pills now. They should still be at the reception.

Rising with some difficulty, she made her way to the doorway, gesturing it open and walking out into the moonlit corridor. Her sight wasn't so great, but the halls were lined with dim lights that helped a lot at night.

Kara made her way to the reception slowly. She got there and saw Al, the guard, immersed in his Holo lenses. As nothing ever actually happened in Tranquility, he could usually be found slacking off.

Retrieving her meds from the labeled dispenser, she started on her way back to her room. As she made her way past the recreation room, however, she noticed a figure seated in the corner of the room, looking out into the moonlit night. Kara couldn't blame her. It was quite the view.

I can stay here for a while. Might help me get my head out of the blender it's been in recently.

She made her way into the room and towards the window. The figure was an elderly woman. She looked about the same age Kara did, and she sat with her arms and legs crossed.

"Hello-"

"Lower your voice," the woman said in a low hiss, not bothering to look away from the window. "They don't like us being outside of our room sensors at night."

"Oh," Kara said in a much lower tone. "I'm sorry."

"It's fine. It's not like you knew, after all. You're not exactly new here, but I certainly haven't seen you night crawling. What's keeping you up tonight?"

"What's keeping *you* up?"

The lady shrugged ever so slightly.

"I have insomnia. What's your excuse?"

"I have a lot on my mind," Kara said. "My head was spinning, and my body ached. Forgot to take *these,*" she continued, holding up her pills. "So, yea. I need to escape this nightmare."

"Nightmare?" She said, finally looking away from the view. "That's a bit harsh. You don't like it here, then?"

Right. I can't tell her I'm from the past. As far as I know, my old brain just doesn't remember what happened the last 64 years.

"That's not what I meant. I was just being dramatic. I'm not used to it here."

"Even after 2 years? Because I've seen you around quite a bit the last 2 years."

Kara faked a little laugh.

"Sorry, my memory isn't what it used to be."

"Ain't that the truth, huh?" her nighttime companion said with a chuckle of her own. It was far more genuine. "I'm Gelisa, by the way."

As she introduced herself, she stretched her hand forward. After about half a second of clueless inaction, Kara shook it.

"I'm Kara. Nice to meet you."

Now that she could see her properly, Kara realized that the woman in front of her looked oddly familiar.

"Hey, you look sort of familiar, Gelisa."

"Like I said, we've been around each other ever so often…"

That's not it. I feel like I remember her from a few days ago. Before all this crazy shit started.

"No, not that," Kara said, thinking hard about it. "Did you by any chance go to Truman High?"

Her face lit up a bit in the moonlight.

"As a matter of fact, I did. Class of 2023. You?"

Damn. What year would it have been again?

"I was class of 2022," Kara responded, after some quick thought. "I must've seen you around at some point. Did you transfer in?"

"Yea. I actually did transfer. AND I went around talking to everybody. We'd just moved from Idaho, and I didn't have any friends."

There was a hint of sadness in her voice. The memory was likely not a pleasant one. But she shook it off and continued.

"Didn't you say your memory was short? It's beyond remarkable that you would remember that."

Stupid move, Kara. I need to be more careful.

"Oh, you know. It was high school. You never really forget high school, do you? It feels like it all happened last week."

"Well, I guess. But I don't remember you at all. I feel kinda bad."

"I don't think we hung out with the same people. I hardly ever met lowerclassmen. Too busy with stuff at home."

"I can believe that. Even here, you hardly ever socialize. This is the longest conversation I've seen you have with *anybody*."

Sounds like even here, I'm still me.

Neither of the two spoke for a few seconds after that.

"I made it awkward, didn't I?" Gelisa said, with an amused look on her face.

"I've done worse."

Kara noticed a photo in Gelisa's hand. It was a younger looking Gelisa with two teenagers by her side.

"Are those your kids?"

"Yeah. They're both lawyers. Very successful, and very busy. You know how it is."

Kara nodded, not really sure how else to respond.

"They were supposed to visit me this week for my birthday, y'know. I was really looking forward to it. But they couldn't make it."

"That's really sad."

"Yeah, well. That's life for ya. It is what it is. Things don't stop moving out there just because we're in here, y'know?"

"Yeah."

"What about you? Got any kids?"

Kara caught herself before she could say no. She still remembered that she'd been told she had a daughter. With all that had been going on, the thought had not come to her often. But now that it had come up, how did she feel about her supposedly estranged daughter?

"I- I don't wanna talk about it."

"Oh," Gelisa said, seemingly embarrassed by her lack of tact. "I'm sorry. I didn't know."

"It- it's fine. It doesn't really matter."

"Hmph. I've been here 15 years, so I know what you mean. It feels like nothing matters anymore. I can't even keep up with the new technology the kids have."

"I know, right?" Kara said, the thought resonating with her immediately. "I saw these goggles the other day that seemed like something out of a Star Trek movie. Remember Star Trek?"

Gelisa laughed out loud.

"I remember. Did you ever think we would become the boomers? Reminiscing and condemning the new technology? Because I sure as hell didn't!"

Kara joined her in her mirth. The irony wasn't lost on her, especially seeing as she was on the other side of the aisle just a few days before.

"Well, the visors I can tell you about. They're mul-tipurpose. Like Smartphones turned up to 11. They do everything, and kids are obsessed with them. You should see how my grandkids throw tantrums when they get their holo lenses taken away."

That sounds awfully familiar.

"Times like that," Gelisa continued, "I miss my husband more, God rest his soul. He was big on discipline, but a big softie everywhere else."

She sighed as the memories resurfaced and rubbed the wedding ring that still occupied her right hand.

"What about yours?"

"Huh?"

"Your husband. Did you ever get married or-?"

"Ummm. No- I mean, yes. I don't remember him too well. It's been a while."

Gelisa seemed puzzled by this.

"You have such a sharp memory but forget the simplest things. You got some sort of Alzheimer's?"

"No! I mean- maybe? I can't remember a large swath of my life. So maybe I do. Is there some way to know for sure?"

"'Course. You can ask that fraud counsellor at the next session. He should be able to set up an analysis or something. I don't know."

Counsellor? Somehow, I don't think that's a good idea. For all I know, the memories I'm looking for aren't even there to begin with. This certainly isn't a dream, but that doesn't mean I'm not right about where I come from.

"I'll ask her to do that, then."

"Him, dear. It's a man."

Crap.

"I can't imagine it. Sure, my husband's gone, and my kids don't visit. But at least I have my memories. You, though…"

"I'll be fine, don't worry."

"That's the spirit. And hey, it's not like you're completely clueless. You seem to have a good grasp of your younger years, eh? Had any siblings?"

"No. It was just my mother and I. Oh, and Da- my stepfather. What about you? Any brothers or sisters?"

"No. I was an only child, same as you. And I liked it that way, for the most part."

A thought that hadn't come to Kara in a while resurfaced.

"I don't know about *that*. I always wanted siblings. But my dad skipped out on us early on, so…"

"Your stepdad didn't want kids?"

"Huh?"

"The man your mother married afterwards. He didn't want any kids."

"I don't know, honestly."

Kara had never thought about that. But she also didn't want to. Dale had invariably caused her current predicament, so she was in no mood to consider his feelings. As she thought this, she noticed that the other lady was giving her a weird look, and then realized she'd been speaking in present tense.

"What I meant to say," Kara added hastily, "was that they never had any, but I don't know if they ever wanted any more. I was a handful."

That seemed to fix things. Gelisa smiled, commenting on how she was also a lot to deal with as a kid.

They spoke back and forth for about another half hour before Gelisa rose to her feet and announced that she was beat and needed to get to bed. Kara had gotten so carried away she hadn't thought that her companion might've been even more tired than she was. As they said their goodbyes and headed off to their rooms, Kara started to feel the fatigue coming on. She'd been starved for any communication at all in the past week or so, and her mind had spared her the droopy eyes and yawns. But now they hit full force.

As she sank into her bed and turned the lights down, Kara couldn't help but smile a bit. She hadn't even remembered to look at the moonlit meadow.

CHAPTER 4

A Chance Encounter

When Kara had been informed of the counselling session, she'd had no idea what to expect from it. But as she sat there, surrounded by strangers and listening to long, heartfelt sob stories, she began to regret not asking. Not that it would have made any difference, mind. The sessions were compulsory.

What's the point of being so bloody old if people still boss you around?

The facilitator was a younger man with short greying hair, a scraggly beard, and a rumpled red button-up shirt. He had been going around, asking each of the residents in attendance questions about themselves and their lives. He was quite boring, and also older than Kara had at first suspected. He was all of 50 years old, but considering his surroundings, that *was* relatively young.

The rest of the class was made up of about 10 other elderly residents, all seated in a circle, with Ben sitting at the head of it.

Kara had been drifting in and out of consciousness the entire time, unable to bear the boredom for long periods of time. It was during one of these spells of awareness that the lady beside her took her turn to speak.

"I never forgave her. And now, I realize that I was just being stubborn and petty. It really was my fault in the end, and I couldn't see it. It's my biggest regret to this day."

Ben had his chin in his hand, seemingly in deep thought. He stayed silent for a moment, then responded in a calm, understanding voice to push the conversation forward.

"Is it really too late to bury the hatchet with her, Mari? Why not reach out and tender your apology? You've certainly realized the error of your ways, and so-"

The lady broke the flow of his words with a loud sobbing.

"Well, she's only gone and died now, hasn't she?! And now I'll never be able to make it right. I'm stuck with this guilt forever."

Despite her hysteria, Ben kept his cool. He stood up and approached her, placing a steady hand on her shoulder and stooping to speak some comforting words. After a few minutes, she seemed to calm down sufficiently, and Ben silently returned to his chair, giving everyone a few moments to recover from the excitement.

"I want everyone to remember, even if someone is no longer with us, it doesn't mean we can't make our peace with them. It's never too late to give yourself the peace of mind you deserve. Everyone makes mistakes, and as long as you've seen the error of your ways, it's not too late."

There was a murmur through the crowd as everyone gave the advice some deep consideration. Everyone except Kara, at least.

"Thank you for that powerful sharing, Mari. I'm sure everyone here was able to relate and learn a thing or two from it. Now, I'm sure we're all eager to finish round the circle and be left alone with our thoughts for a while. So, who's next?"

Kara was well aware that it was her turn to *drop her burdens*, as Ben called it. But as she certainly couldn't tell them what was on her mind, she ignored the call. Instead she looked around like she really didn't know that it was her turn.

"Kara? Would you like to share with us? I've seen you around, and you always look like you've got something on your chest. I'm interested to know what it is."

Should've excused myself while I had the chance.

Kara faced the circle, no longer able to feign ignorance.

"Um, I'd rather not talk about it. It's really personal, and sort of hopeless."

Ben fixed his unusually steady gaze on Kara once more, making her feel like she was being dissected.

"If it's too personal for group time, we can always schedule a private session with just the two of us. Or, if you prefer, I can send over a qualified female associate of mine. She might help you be more at ease one on one."

Before Kara could say anything, Ben tilted his head ever so slightly, like he was struggling to remember something.

"Ah, yes. There's also the small issue of your memory loss. I was informed that you had a bit of an episode a week or so ago. Would you care to fill us in on it?" he said. And then, turning to the class, he continued, "Memory loss is something we all struggle with, I'm sure. It's nothing to be ashamed of and we can all learn a thing or two from Kara's experience with it."

Fuck.

Kara had been worried that this would come up. She had no idea what sort of treatments the doctors in this timeline had for memory loss. What if they were able to see that there were no memories there in the first place? She had no way to excuse her state of mind, nor did she have an explanation to give for how things got this way.

"Oh, that. I'd rather not discuss it. It's fine now. I'm much better and I've apologized to the nurses I spooked."

Ben shifted his posture to a more laid back one, releasing his fingers from their intertwined positions and softening his gaze. This was obviously his attempt to foster a more relaxing atmosphere.

"Oh, I know you're better now. But that doesn't mean we can't discuss it for the benefit of others as well as yourself. This is a safe place where you can let it all out. I'm sure the ordeal was even more frightening for you than it was for your nurses."

A few murmurs rose up from the rest of the class, likely some form of encouragement or the other.

"Your fellow residents clearly want to give you a listening ear, it seems. Don't keep them waiting, Kara."

Kara's mind darted this way and that, looking for a response of any sort. More delay tactics, a lie, some old story she could pass off as recent. Anything.

But nothing came up. The more she searched, the more her mood fouled, and her patience wore thin. She struggled to keep her cool, knowing that it would be best to avoid trouble with Ben or anyone else that could have her examined.

"Don't be shy, dearie."

The lady beside her had seemingly recovered from her own despair and was trying to help Kara along. But it had the opposite effect.

"You know what? This is stupid. Everybody goes through some stuff, right? What's the point of sitting here like a bunch of kids in preschool and talking about them? We're grownups. And blabbing about your issues in public is lame."

A heavy silence settled on the group as she said this, and all eyes fixed on her. Around the room, other residents that had taken their turn at group earlier and were still around enjoying the ambiance stopped and looked at Kara as well.

Maybe that was a bit too loud. Just a bit.

Ben was quick to regain his composure. He cleared his throat and rose to his feet, instantly drawing all the attention back to himself.

"It's okay. Thank you, Kara. I can sense that's truly how you feel. And that's why we're here. To express how we feel."

The others in the circle seemed to be put off by this, and a few made their distaste heard.

Ben registered this, and as he continued, he raised a single finger to his face and wagged it lazily. A small smile appeared on his lips as he continued.

"But just because her feelings are valid doesn't mean she's doing things the right way. And while we must admire her confidence, we must also note that her approach is unhealthy."

Some more murmurs, this time in support of him.

"So, Kara," he said, focusing on her once more, "I respect your feelings on the matter. But I must reiterate that this is a safe space, where we do not pass judgement. You can make your distaste known without mocking those who choose to do things the right way. Because in the end, it takes courage to speak up about the parts of ourselves that we would rather hide. Being open is a sign of strength. Never forget that. And that's all we have time for this week, everyone."

The crowd awarded his eloquence and manner with a hearty round of applause, which was rare for the old folk there.

Well, he'd certainly make a good cult leader.

As the group dispersed and Kara started to make her way out, Ben approached her.

"Kara! Wait up."

Kara stopped, rolling her eyes as she turned to speak to him. She'd learnt very quickly that trying to get anywhere quickly was a no-go.

Curse these old bones.

"I sense that you're going through a lot, despite what you say. If you ever feel like having that one on one session, I'd be happy to come over or send someone more suitable in my stead."

This fucking guy…

"Thank you. I'll consider it."

Kara said this with a smile and a wave, but she was sure anyone with even the most basic ability to read people would know she was faking.

"That's all I ask."

He gave a quick bow and went on his way.

Kara went on her way, resolving to remove her name form the participation list for the group sessions and possibly file a restraining order on Ben. She laughed at the latter, knowing she was being unfair. He couldn't know what she was going through. In his defense, he was clearly just trying to help, just as he had helped a ton of others before her. Wouldn't stop her from removing her name though.

She set off in the direction of the recreation room, as the reception was in that area.

*****

"Hello. How may I help you, young lady?"

Jacqui stood over the visitor in the lobby of the reception with her lunch in hand. She had been rushing off to find a quiet place to eat before the next activity. Since the residents couldn't exactly eat whatever they wanted, there was a rule about where staff could eat their own food. Lunch was especially stressful, as Jacqui couldn't go all the way back to her quarters and leave the residents totally unattended.

In her haste to get somewhere more suitable she had almost missed the long-haired teen seated alone at the reception area.

Almost.

But she didn't. The girl was around 16, dressed like she was 20 in a building full of people between the ages of 40 to 95. So, Jacqui had stopped her lunch rush short to attend to her.

"Oh, hello ma'am. I'm Vera. I called about meeting my grandmother yesterday."

The girl's smile was immense, but Jacqui couldn't bring herself to return it. She'd heard from one of the call staff that someone had called in to see Laura Chambers and introduced herself as her long-lost granddaughter. The problem was that Laura Chambers had unfortunately passed away a few years ago. This Vera girl apparently didn't know, and neither did the call staff, apparently.

"Oh dear. Ummm… Why don't you go into the rec. room over there, sweetie? The music's out of date but it's definitely better than sitting here all on your own. Someone will be with you shortly."

"Okay. Thanks!"

The young girl walked briskly towards the rec room, and Jacqui breathed a sigh of relief. She couldn't think of anything she wanted less than to be the one to break the bad news to the girl.

*I wonder who **does** have reception duty, actually?* She thought to herself as she walked over to the desk and hit the buzzer twice.

"Hello?" a voice said over the intercom built into the desk.

"Travis, is that you? There's a bit of a problem. I'm gonna need you to get back here ASAP."

"Roger that, ma'am. I'll be there in a minute."

"Oh, and Travis?" she added, hearing the faint sound of chewing. "Please tell me where you're having lunch. I'm starving."

******

I'm more than just an option
(Hey, hey, hey)
Refuse to be forgotten
(Hey, hey, hey)
I took a chance with my heart
(Hey, hey, hey)
And I feel it taking over
I better find your lovin'
I better find your heart
I better find your lovin'
I better find your heart

Kara sat alone at her table, listening to the music. She remembered it well, as it had only been a few months since she'd last heard it. The other residents, however, seemed overcome with nostalgia.

"This song always got me in the feels, Robbie."

Kara cast a fleeting look at the resident one table down from where she was. He was the one speaking, rather loudly, to his friend.

"Yea, Jake. Drake was always the ticket. Back in the day, his songs got me all sorts of ladies."

"Ah. It was the movies for me. Two tickets, two popcorns and one ride to my place. Yes sir. At least until all we got was remakes. Remember that?"

"I remember! There were no good movies for almost 5 years. At least, not till the superhero flicks. Ah, those were the good 'ole days."

Kara's frown deepened on hearing this. Just weeks ago, she'd been complaining about remakes to her friends and now she had solid evidence that the trend would carry on. If she ever made it back, she was boycotting the cinema forever.

That's a big if, though.

"…a chip in your head, like built in google, I tell ya."

"Ohhh. Google. Whatever happened to those guys?"

"OmniSearch bought 'em out a decade ago. Keep up with the times, Lou."

After she had made a mental note of the name of the company, the background conversations held no real interest for Kara, and she found herself drifting in her own thoughts once more.

Until…

"Nana?"

The voice was much closer than the others and snapped Kara out of her daze. She looked up to see a long-haired youngster in trendy clothes standing on the other side of her table with a questioning look on her face.

Did she just call me nana?

Not knowing how to respond, Kara decided to ignore her and see if she'd move on.

"Is that you, Nana?"

Kara sighed internally, turning to the girl and putting on her best old lady impression.

"And who might you be, young lady?"

"I... I think I'm your granddaughter."

"Oh my. I don't think I have any grandkids, dearie."

The girl seemed unperturbed, and pulled out a picture from her pocket, unfolding it and placing it in front of Kara ever so gently. In it, there was a young woman who looked very much like an older version of the girl standing in front of her now, and beside that…

"Is that…me?"

She smiled wide, and Kara could see a hint of tears in her narrowed eyes. She shrugged with her hands up and said;

"Surprise?"

*****

"So basically, my mom, Emma, was your daughter. She had me, but gave me up for adoption soon after she had me."

Kara was seated across from the young girl in the rec room, her head abuzz with incomprehensible emotions. Her name was Vera, and she had come looking for her grandmother.

She'd come looking for Kara.

"Was?"

"Ummm, yeah." Vera's enthusiasm seemed to fall for a moment. "She passed away not too long ago."

The news further complicated the storm of emotion raging within Kara. She'd heard that her relationship with her daughter had been strained for years. But even at that, she felt a dark hand grasp at her heart.

How can I care about a kid I don't remember having? Why do I feel so dead inside?

"I know it's a lot to take in. I just found all this out a few weeks ago, myself."

Vera spoke in a soothing voice, trying to make the whole thing easier on Kara.

I'm probably not making her feel any better with my silence.

Kara had no idea what to think about any of this. On the one hand, she'd never been married or had kids that she could remember. The mind and heart in this old body of hers had never experienced any of it. But on the other hand, Kara couldn't deny that seeing Vera and hearing her story had resonated with something deep within her that she'd previously never known either.

"Nana?"

"Vera. Hi."

"I'm sorry if this whole situation isn't a welcome one. I was just so excited to-"

"Don't be silly! I'm so glad you found me."

Kara stretched out her arms to embrace her new-found grandkid. Vera hesitated, but only for a second. She wrapped Kara in the warmest embrace she'd ever felt.

"Hey, do you wanna take a walk together or something?"

Kara didn't know exactly why she was being so accommodating. Still, thinking about it, she realized she didn't want to question it. Somewhere inside of herself, Kara had come to the realization that she was probably stuck here in a body several decades closer to the end than she'd been a month ago. The thought was depressing, but there was pretty much nothing she could do.

Vera may be the only family I ever know.

"Yes, I'd love to."

*****

Kara had never actually taken a walk around the premises of the nursing home. Even though she'd been enthralled by the beauty of the garden, there were far more pressing distractions within the walls of her new home. But as she strode through the lush greenery with Vera in tow, she found her mind clear of negative emotions once again.

Vera had been filling Kara in on her life up till now, and she'd listened with quite a bit of interest.

"-and I'm still in high school right now. And it sorta sucks. There's a ton of drama and stuff. And when I go off to college, I wanna study medicine. Just like my adoptive parents."

"Wow. That's great, Vera. But isn't that a tough course to get into?"

"Yeah. It actually is. I'll probably need a perfect UAT score to even be considered for admission. But I know it'll be worth it. I've always liked helping people."

Kara considered asking what a UAT score was but decided to just treat it like the SATs. That seemed to be the context, anyway.

"I can see that you're that kind of person. You're sweet and very respectful. Especially for your age."

"Especially for my age? What do you mean, Nana?"

"Oh, nothing. It's just that I remember when I was in high school like it was yesterday. And I remember things being quite different back in my day."

"Really? What was it like?"

"Well, we were far less polite, for one. My friends and I were more interested in partying and hanging out than helping people. I don't think I even once considered that. But people change as they grow older, of course," Kara added, seeing the amused look on Vera's face.

"I know, I know."

"But, it's admirable that you're already so focused."

"Not really," Vera said, blushing a little. "I think everyone my age is like that. The attitude changes with the times, I guess."

Kara nodded, but she had her doubts. She still plainly remembered her first day in the cafeteria and how another teen roughly Vera's age had acted. She'd seen more of them since then, all with varying degrees of nonchalance and rude behavior. Not a single one had been as pleasant as Vera was.

The two sat down on a beautifully crafted park bench, looking over a small pond. The fish in it seemed to change color as they swam around in the crystal-clear water.

"So, what kind of music did you listen to, Nana?"

"Well, a little bit of everything, really. I'm really into-"

"Hey!"

Kara and Vera turned to see who had said that and were surprised to see Jacqui standing behind them. Between their conversation and the gentle serenity of their pondside environment, they hadn't noticed her walking up to meet them.

"Good evening, ladies."

"Hello, ma'am. Nice to see you again."

Jacqui returned Vera's greeting with a smile, then turned her attention to Kara.

"Mrs. Smith, may I borrow you for a moment?"

Kara had no idea what this was about. She'd been enjoying the calm and conversation, but figured that Jacqui wouldn't pull her away unless it was urgent. She gave a quick nod and rose laboriously to her feet, following Jacqui away towards the main building.

"Sorry about that. But you need to take your ITP pill before 7, and you tend to forget so-"

"Oh, okay. That shouldn't take too long. I'd really like to get back to Vera."

Jacqui gave Kara a weird sideways glance and slowed down to speak to her.

"What's that all about?"

"Nothing. Just spending some quality time with my granddaughter."

"Your… granddaughter."

"Yea. Is there a problem?"

Jacqui sighed and facepalmed softly.

"Mrs. Smith, she's not your granddaughter."

The words hit Kara like a car bumper on a lonely inner street.

"What? But she said-"

"I know what she probably thought. Looking at the records, I can see that her grandma bore an uncanny resemblance to you. But the poor girl doesn't know her real family. Her grandmother was Laura. Laura Chambers."

"Laura- Wait, *was?*"

Another sigh escaped Jacqui as they reached the medicine dispensary.

"Yea. Was. She died a while back, see. Right after she heard her daughter had passed away. She didn't take the news well," Jacqui explained, handing Kara a large yellow pill. "Here, take this. Like I was saying, she didn't take it so well, so-"

"Well, neither will Vera. Jesus Christ, I- she just- She's so happy right now, you know? This is gonna hurt her a ton."

"What do you mean?"

"Well, first she finds out that her biological mom is dead, and then thinks she'd found her grandma. And now she's gonna find out that it was all a misunderstanding and she's dead too. That sounds like it would be devastating."

"Oh."

Jacqui looked at Kara with a weird expression on her face as the latter swallowed the sweetened pill. It looked a suspicious lot like a scheming face.

"Well, Mrs. Smith. You seem an awful lot invested in young Vera's case. Why don't I leave it to you to break the news to her? The Head Medical Officer was supposed to, but he was called up for an emergency operation. He won't be free for another day or two."

Kara made no response. She hid it well, but deep down, she felt sadness crushing back down, like when she'd woken up on that first night. All the positive energy that had come with Vera's revelation seemed to evaporate into thin air.

"Mrs. Smith? Hello?"

"Oh. Umm, yeah. I'll break it to her. It's the least I could do."

"That's good. You don't have to do it immediately. Pick a time you feel is convenient and run with it. I'm sure she'll feel a bit better if it comes from you. If I've learned anything from my time here, it's that bad news given the right way isn't so bad."

"Jacqui, she's 16. There's no good way for her to take this."

Jacqui seemed to think about it for a minute, then nodded and placed a hand on Kara's shoulder.

"Good luck, ma'am."

*****

When Kara got back to the pond area, Vera was still seated, but with a small island of food spread out on the bench.

"Well, that wasn't here before."

"Yeah. I brought lunch. I imagine that the food here isn't great."

"Some of the stuff on that menu is really… special," Kara said, thinking back to the first meal she'd had. "Let's just say I'm grateful for all the cuisine tablets we get."

"Oh, yeah. Those are good. I had a few once at the state fair. You get those every day?"

"Yea. A different kind every meal, but only one at a time."

"Well," Vera said, offering Kara a sandwich, "This isn't a cuisine tab, but it's pretty good."

The two sat in silence for a while, enjoying the sand-wiches. Then Vera opened up the rest of the packed lunch, and Kara decided that she was ready and willing to suffer whatever consequences old people had for overeating. There was a little bit of every-thing, from chicken slices to avocado toast. A 6 pack of tiny juice boxes that said sugar-free at the bottom came next, and Kara had never tasted anything like them in her life.

As the two reclined on the bench, both very satisfied and tranquil, Vera reached out and held Kara's hand without looking.

"Nana?"

"Yes, Vera?"

"Do you have a lot of friends here? Like, people your age?"

"I don't know why, but you feel like a long-lost friend. I mean, I'd expected to have some sort of connection, but it's so much more than I could have imagined. Talking to you has been some of the best time I've spent in ages. I can't wait for us to get to know each other better."

"About that. I would love to spend much more time with you, but-"

"Oh, it's okay, Nana. I already know how strict the visiting rules here are. That's why I asked my big brother to move you out so you can come live with us. I just got off the phone with him before you got back, and he's ecstatic about the idea. That is, if you want to."

Kara looked at Vera, and her heart melted from the sight of her. Her expression was one of longing, reaching out to her. Even with the knowledge that they weren't related, Kara still felt the connection to her.

It was like the universe itself had brought them together.

Even as the absurdity of the idea outlined itself clearly in her head, Kara could feel her spirit pushing, egging her to take Vera up on her offer.

*What do I have to lose? What does she? We need each other, and we've found each other here. I can't explain it, but I'm drawn to her like she really **is** family. And it would be the best thing I could think of to get out of here.*

Her mind had lost, as her heart won out, and her conscience sat on the fence of her internal dialogue, as it had often done last summer, all those decades ago.

"Wait, you said your brother, right? What about your parents? Won't they-"

"They're gone. My adoptive parents that is. They died last year. There was an accident, just before my aunt's wedding. A lot of family members didn't make it. Telling the truth about my adoption was my mom's deathbed confession."

I have to say no. I have to tell her the truth…

But I can't.

"Okay. Let's do it."

CHAPTER 5

Trading Up

"Good evening to you too, sir. Yes, I'd like to check my grandmother out right now, please. Is there any paperwork we have to do before she can leave? I'd like to get back home within my curfew if I can."

Kara sat in the nursing home's reception area, waiting and watching as Vera was handed a tablet that looked like an even thinner iPad. She seemed to fill out some details, sign off on the form, and then pass her student ID in front of a built-in scanner.

"Ma'am, this way, please. We need to do a quick examination before we can let you leave with your granddaughter."

The male nurse on desk duty stood beside his work station, waiting for Kara to step forward. His Medic-Droid was hovering beside him, seemingly waiting to aid in administering whatever checkup she needed. She rose and approached the table briskly. While her feelings had overruled her common sense, she strongly suspected that Jacqui would be more responsible. And she really didn't want to get caught.

"Hold out your hand, please. This will only take a second. So, are you willingly going to stay with this young lady?"

"Yes, of course. I already said that, didn't I?"

"Sorry, ma'am. Formal confirmation is all. Just doing my job. Your hand, please?"

Kara complied, and the little droid let out a bright beam that seemed to scan her torso a few times. It made a short, beeping noise and returned to the nurse.

"Okay, you seem about as good as you did at your last checkup. Your medication will be delivered to you every other week, and your meals will be dropped off every morning."

The nurse looked up and let out a small laugh at the horrified look on Kara's face.

"That's just a little joke I like to tell. You *are* entitled to your three meals a day, seeing as you paid for your stay in advance, Mrs. Smith. But no one ever actually takes that option, and I don't think we even bother keeping a food delivery guy around."

"That's fine. Anything else?"

"No, lass. I just need a signature from her personal overseer. I've already sent the request. Should only be a few minutes now."

When Kara realized what he had said, fear shot through her faster than she could blink.

If he tells Jacqui, she's gonna ruin everything! What do I do?

"So," Kara said, fighting to keep her voice calm and even." All you need is Jacqui's permission, and we can leave, right?"

"Oh, no ma'am. Miss J is not your overseer. It's Miss Barabara. And-"the nurse said as he paused to look down at his MedicDroid. "she just signed off on it. With a note to you, missy." he added, gesturing to Vera.

"Oh. Okay."

"She says; *take care of your Nana. She's got a really youthful attitude, but she needs to take things easy.*"

"Well, youthful is right. Isn't it, Nana?"

"You bet."

Words could not begin to describe how relieved Kara felt at the news that Jacqui had not been notified. Her entire plan had briefly come undone, and she couldn't wait till she was out the door.

"Okay. That's that. I hope you have a wonderful time. Take this, if you would." the nurse said, handing Kara a bracelet. It looked like it was made of the same weird material that the walls were made of. "That's a monitoring bracelet. It keeps track of your vitals and will notify us, as well as the household's first aid droid, of any basic issues that may arise. There's also a panic button on there. You don't have to wear it, but we strongly advise that you do. You'll always have a place here, mainly because you paid for it, so feel free to return if you so wish."

"Thanks, I guess."

Kara slipped the band into the pocket of the joggers that she'd changed into, with no intention of wearing it ever. As she had no regular clothes or personal effects outside of the ones the nursing home had provided, Vera had taken her to the shopping center and gotten her a few casual outfits *for starters.* So now she was in a plain white T-shirt and comfy joggers over some loose slippers.

I might still be old, but at least now I'm not dressed like someone's grandma. Ironic that it would happen now that I ***am*** *someone's grandma.*

"Ready to get outta here, Nana?"

"Yes. Yes, I am."

"Shall I call you a cab, ladies? If you remain seated for a bit, one will be right along."

The nurse was holding up his desk phone and gesturing towards the chairs in the reception area.

"No, that's okay. I drove here, so we have a ride. But thanks anyway."

With that, Vera picked up the shopping bags with Kara's new clothes in them and started towards the door. Kara looked over the reception area one last time and then turned on her heels and left.

"You have your own car, Vera?" Kara asked as she caught up with her new granddaughter, who had slowed down to let her meet up.

"Yea. It was a gift from Jeff for my sweet sixteen."

"Jeff?"

"Yea. My older brother. He's my legal guardian now."

A thought came to Kara as she walked side by side with Vera.

"Your adopted older brother, you mean?"

"Well," Vera said, taking a moment to think. "yeah, he is. But family's family, so it doesn't really matter. You'll see."

I doubt it, Kara thought to herself as they walked further down the street. Kara had never been out the front entrance that led to the outside world before, and the experience was ruined by her terrible vision. It wasn't all that bad compared to some of the other residents. Still, it did prevent her from seeing much outside of the streetlight beams that illuminated the center of the road.

"We're here! Wanna ride shotgun?"

Vera stood in front of a pink, sleek looking car, fumbling with the bags in her hand to get to the keys to open the doors. She managed to get it out and pressed a button on it. With a beep, the car door unlocked and slid upwards with a low hiss. As Vera tossed the bags behind the driver's seat and made her way around the hood to help her into the passenger's side, Kara squinted and caught a glimpse of the logo emblazoned on the futuristic-looking steering wheel.

"Wait. This is *your* car??"

"Yea. You don't like it, Nana?"

"Vera, it's a Ferrari. You have a Ferrari."

"Yeah, it is. I wouldn't have chosen something quite so flashy, but Jeff puts a lot of stock in the beauty of things."

Vera laughed a bit after saying this, and Kara felt like a joke had just gone over her head. But she was far too enamored by the car to care. When she had seen the exterior, she'd been very impressed, but had simply assumed that all cars would look like this in the future. But as they left the gated community that housed the nursing home and got on the better lit freeway, Kara realized she'd been wrong.

Most of the cars on the road looked pretty much the same as they did in her time, with just a few strange features. They were all generally better looking, but none of them could hold a candle to the one she was seated in. As she processed this, her mind wandered back to the shopping center, and how Vera had practically emptied it out and paid without batting an eye. Kara had assumed this had something to do with clothes being way cheaper in the future, but now she wasn't so sure.

Her brother must be loaded.

Kara hadn't considered what sort of place she'd be moving into and had agreed solely because of the connection she felt to Vera. But now it seemed she was in for a relaxing time.

They won't get any complaints from me.

Kara glanced over at Vera, who had been driving without a hitch the entire time, and found her stealing glances at her every few seconds. She had a massive smile on her face and almost seemed to radiate joy.

"Whoa. Keep your eyes on the road, Vera. You're creeping me out a little."

"Sorry. Sorry. I'm just so excited to finally meet you. And now we're gonna be living together!"

"You'll see enough of me every day when you get back from school."

"Get back?"

"Do you not go to school?"

"Well, yeah. But it's all virtual. No one's gone to a physical school since a few years after the whole 2020 debacle".

"What happened in 2020?"

Vera seemed to wince at the thought of it.

"We don't talk about that."

*****

"Did you take a wrong turn somewhere, Vera?"

Vera laughed a bit.

"No, Nana."

"So we're at the right place? This is where you live?"

"That's right. Come on, let's go inside. Don't want you catching a cold."

Even after asking, Kara couldn't be entirely sure she wasn't being pranked. The house that stood before them was a mansion. It was not a large townhouse or anything like that. It was a real, larger than life playboy style mansion. The building was huge, and she couldn't see anything past it. Still, the gated property they now stood in was larger than the entirety of the nursing home, with a brilliant white fence topped with gold spearheads. There was a lush, expansive lawn with grass figures and lights and automatic sprinklers. The structure itself looked like it was two stories tall, and it seemed to be built like a traditional colonial, but as she got closer, Kara realized that it was made of different material and had been *made* to look like that.

This is beyond just rich. They're probably millionaires. Or worse.

"The lights are on in the entrance, so I'm guessing Jeff's home."

Kara's worries came flooding back at the mention of his name. Surely anyone would object to an unrelated old lady waltzing into their home.

He isn't even related to Vera, for fuck's sake. This is a terrible idea.

Vera knocked twice on the large wooden doors, and they swung inwards. A man in what was clearly butler's garb stood in front of them and bowed as he stepped aside to reveal the most beautiful room Kara had ever seen.

Directly across the room, a grand stairway branched both ways at the first landing, which had portraits of various family members. Directly above was a crystal chandelier the size of a small couch. The light it gave off was supplemented by the same ambient light built into the nursing home walls. The floors were tiled with white marble squares splashed with red like an impressionist painting, and an elegant rug took up a large swath of the space between the stairwell and the door.

"Welcome, grandmother!"

Kara's attention was brought back to the present by a deep, booming voice hailing her from the doorway of an adjacent room. She turned to look and found a midsized man in his late 20s striding confidently towards her. He was in a three-piece suit and Italian shoes that shone like metal. As he approached her, something circled him at high speeds and came to settle in his palm. Kara recognized it as a Medic-Droid, and she vaguely remembered Vera mentioning her parents being doctors.

Guess the apple doesn't fall far from the tree.

He got to her and gave her a hug so tight it started to hurt.

"Oww."

"Oh, sorry."

He let go of her and shot a winning smile in her direction. He was obviously a very social person.

"I'm Jeff, Vera's brother. And your new grandson, if you'll let me. "

"Nice to meet you, Jeff. I'm Kara."

"Can I call you Nana?"

"Umm… sure. If you want to."

"Splendid!"

Another person came out from the room where Jeff had been. She was in her late teens, with a tall and thin frame, model features, and a blindingly white smile. Her red velvet dress went down as far as her thin waist before sheering off in two directions. It was the most daring slit Kara had ever seen on a dress.

"Ah, Miss. Robinson! I'm sorry for the delay. I'd like you to meet my grandmother. She's just now arrived from the nursing home. Nana," Jeff said.

Turning to Kara, he continued.

"Nana, this is Ms. Robinson, one of my patients. I was just finishing her debrief from her latest procedure when we heard the doors open."

"Nice to meet you, ma'am," the woman said, stretching a hand towards Kara. As she shook the lady's hand, it occurred to Kara that she spoke in a way that sounded much older than her actual age.

"Anyway, Jeff, I was just coming to tell you I'm leaving. My husband and the kids need me home for dinner."

"Husband?" Kara said, shocked. "Aren't you a little too young to be married?"

At this, everyone around her gave a hearty laugh. That was, other than the butler, who stood stoic as ever as the rest of them laughed up a small storm.

Oh no. Did I say something wrong? Is it normal to be married at 19 in the future?

"Wow," Jeff said, recovering from his laughter first. "I've received a lot of praise over the years, but I think that's my favorite comment so far, Nana. Thank you."

"Huh?"

"You see, Mrs. Robinson here is one of my patients at my practice. I'm a plastic surgeon, and I've been working to make her look younger. She's actually 45, and a mother of two at that."

Kara's jaw dropped, and the room filled with cheery laughter once more.

"Well, I'm also very impressed by Jeff's work. He only gets better with time, honestly. Worth the high cost, surely."

"I aim to please, ma'am."

There was a bit of small talk, and then Mrs. Robinson took her leave, escorted by the butler.

"Pleasant lady. So, Vera, how was your day with Nana?"

"It was sooo much fun! She's awesome."

"I'm sure. I hope you won't miss the nursing home too much, Nana. There's not a lot of people your age around here to hang out with, but we'll do our very best to make sure you're taken care of. It's gonna be-"

There was a beeping sound from Jeff's MedicDroid, and he picked it up, looking at the screen. The smile on his face dulled a bit, and he looked back at Vera and Kara, disappointed.

"I'd love to talk so much more, but I've just received an urgent message. There's a shareholder meeting at one of dad's hospitals, and my PA forgot to put it on my schedule. Anyway, I'm sure you're exhausted right now, so we'll pick this up tomorrow, okay?"

Kara nodded slowly, and before she could say anything, he'd spun on his heels and marched off.

"So, what'd you think?" Vera asked, beaming at Kara.

Kara was still at a loss for words, and returned Vera's smile, albeit weakly.

"He's really… something, all right."

Vera laughed cheerily at her response.

"Yeah. He's a bit extra, but you get used to it. He's a great brother, and he'll be a great grandson, too."

Kara still had her doubts, but kept them to herself. With all the excitement of the day, she was exhausted, and the feeling hit her squarely then. Vera noticed and decided they'd had enough excitement for one day.

"Hey, Nana. Are you hungry?"

"No, I'm still stuffed from our picnic earlier. Why?"

"Just checking. Anyway, we should probably get to bed now, yeah?"

"Sure."

Nothing sounded as good as a nice, long rest to Kara right then. There was a lot swimming through her mind, and it was beginning to wear on her. She'd complicated her already bizarre situation even more by lying and following Vera to this place. The nursing home would probably rat her out as soon as Jacqui found out she was gone, and there would be consequences. But it hadn't been her usual bad streak that had led her here. She'd felt a real connection to Vera, and coming here with her had felt the natural thing to do.

If there's one thing I'm not great at, it's fighting my nature. Let's just hope it doesn't get me into something I can't escape. Well, any more than it already has.

"-room is just around the corner. I figured you'd probably be better off without the stairs. So, ready to go to bed?"

Vera's voice broke through her thoughts, and Kara returned back to her very tired consciousness.

"Yes, dear," she answered. "Lead the way."

CHAPTER 6

Kindness and Choices

After a month at the mansion, Kara still struggled not to get lost in the massive structure's rooms and passageways. It was as if the more she explored, the more of it there was to get lost in. This particular morning, she'd somehow found her way into a strange room filled from wall to wall with the type of mannequins she assumed biology labs would have. They were cross-sectioned in various ways, with accurate depictions of their insides.

Freaky. But then again, you'd sort of expect this from a family of doctors. No wonder Vera wants to study medicine.

She'd wandered around it for a while until the butler found her, as he so often did. He'd led her to the dining area, where Vera and Jeff had been waiting for her. She'd narrated her journey through the unknown, and they'd had a good laugh about it together, and an excellent breakfast to boot. Not that there was any meal that was a miss here. Having a personal chef that wasn't your mom apparently had its perks. Then Jeff had rushed off someplace as he always did. Kara was left alone with Vera to discuss syrup versus honey on pancakes until it was time for the young girl to go take her online class in her room.

Now, hours later, as Kara sat alone in her own enormous room, she could barely concentrate on the TV show she was watching. Whenever she was alone like this, she'd find herself lost in her own thoughts again. And staying here had undoubtedly given her a lot to think about.

First of all, not only had Jacqui apparently not so much as uttered a word to Vera about Kara's deception, the nursing home had continued to send her medication and monitor her through the health bracelet, which Jeff had begged her to wear as much as she could.

I may technically be a doctor, but you'll be in much better hands if others with more experience caring for people your age handled things for us, he'd said. But so far, she'd been alright. Other than some minor pains that were more or less normal for people her age, she'd been doing much better overall.

But more nagging than the mystery of Jacqui's silence was the behavior of Jeff and Vera themselves. Their relationship had puzzled Kara since the very day she'd gotten here. At first, she'd had her doubts about Jeff. There was no reason why he'd take in a relative of Kara's. After all, they weren't even related to begin with. And he'd certainly have his reservations about Vera herself, too. Good guy or not, there had to be a limit to his love for a biological stranger, right?

She'd been wrong. In the time she'd been there, Jeff had surprised her with his behavior. Not only did he treat Vera with every ounce of love and care imaginable, but his irrationality also spread to the way he treated her as well. Despite not being related to her even in lies, Jeff had treated her like a mother to him. She had everything she could dream of, and he'd find a few minutes every day between meetings and appointments to come in and check on her. It was almost like he'd convinced himself they were actually a family.

Weird.

Pulling herself out of her own mind, Kara decided to see what was on TV. Vera had initially had it set on The Throwback Network, which exclusively featured shows from Kara's teen years. At first, it had seemed incredible, but Kara had slowly come to resent the content. There was something about her current situation that gave her a different lens with which to view the shows. They seemed shallow to her, more noise than a symphony. The last straw had come from her former favorite, a prank show called The Bad Mannered. She'd almost squealed with regular girlish excitement when it had been announced as coming up next. By the time the opening sequence played, she'd been singing its praises to Vera, who was with her in her room that night, for over an hour.

But it had been a letdown of epic proportions.

Somehow, the *hilarious* prospect of teenagers pulling mean-spirited pranks on the elderly seemed to have lost its appeal to Kara. By the third submission on the episode, Kara had had enough. She turned to Vera to request she change the channel and was surprised to find her visibly angered.

"This isn't funny at all. This is abuse of the elderly! How could they let them get away with this? And while filming no less. Was this what all your shows were like back then, Nana?"

"No. Not all of them."

Kara said this in good faith, but deep down, she realized that her taste in shows had likely undergone a drastic change now that she was no longer a teen. And she had been right. It wasn't just pranking shows. Soaps, Comedy specials, even My Lie under the Mistletoe, her favorite Christmas special. All her favorite shows suddenly seemed offensive and mean spirited. The change rattled her significantly. Less than three months ago, these shows were her most treasured moments of the week.

But now she wasn't the same person anymore.

"TV, activate."

The gigantic monitor slid out from behind a holographic panel in the far wall of her room, and the screen came on, showing a still image of her first lunch with Vera and Jeff that the butler had taken. The picture was amazing on the TV, but then so was everything else on it. The first time she'd seen it, Kara had been amazed by just how enormous it was, and the shock and awe were still there, even a month later. Why anyone even needed a 180-inch display was beyond her. Not that she was complaining. The pictures in it looked more precise than what her regular eyes could see by a longshot.

"TV, next channel."

The channel switched from the still image to a live sports broadcast, which Kara had no interest in. Somewhere in the last few decades, all her favorite sports had been overhauled or replaced to incorporate new technology and interests. Some of them were quite exciting, but it just wasn't the same.

She changed the channel, flipping through till she found a nature documentary, and watched it till her eyes got heavy and her mind clouded…

*****

"Hey, Nana!"

Kara woke up with a start, her eyes darting around till they settled on Vera's face looking down on her from above.

"Oh, hello, dear."

"You fell asleep with the TV on again," she said, pointing over her shoulder at the nature doc that was just concluding with closing credits.

"Oh, sorry about that. I must've wasted a ton of power."

Vera laughed a bit.

"You can't *really* waste power, Nana. It's clean and renewable now. I'm just worried the noise will disturb your rest."

"I'm a heavier sleeper than that."

"I guess you are. Anywayyy," Vera continued, looking extremely pleased with herself. "I have some great news. The shelter where I volunteer has an opening now! There's usually a crowding limit, but Mrs. Martinez moved away with her new family, so now you can come with until the manager finds a replacement!"

Kara had no idea what Vera was going on about, and her facial expression clearly showed it.

"Huh?"

"Oh, right. I should probably slow down a notch. See, I volunteer at this shelter downtown on Saturdays and Sundays, and there's usually a limit to how many volunteers can be there at a time. And since we all come round every week, there's almost never a chance to bring anyone with. But now I can bring you tomorrow to volunteer with me. It's gonna be great. We can spend the day together and give back at the same time."

Kara forced a weak smile, but internally she was having some serious reservations about the entire thing. She was aware that Vera did some work every week, but hadn't realized that it was charity stuff.

Volunteer work? I didn't like that even when I could do stuff without my body constantly aching like a wrestler after a show. And I sure as hell don't feel like giving anything back right now. But I can't exactly say no to Vera, can I? Gotta suck it up and go, I guess. She just wants me there. I probably don't have to do much.

But even as she thought this through, there was a nagging voice at the back of her head that questioned why she was so against a little charity work. Vera seemed to enjoy it, and she was a great girl. What did that say about her at that age, which was just a few weeks ago?

"I'd love that," Kara said, steeling herself. "What time do we leave?"

Vera beamed at her with the same toothy grin she always had.

"It's pretty early, Nana. So we should probably go get dinner now so you can get to bed early, yeah?"

Such a happy little thing. But then who wouldn't be happy in her position?'

"Dinner sounds good. Let's go."

*****

The next morning, Kara woke up feeling severely conflicted. As she made her way down for breakfast, she decided that there was nothing she could do but try her best.

Well, it's still dark out. So I at least have some time to-

"Morning, Nana!"

"Fuc- I mean, hey Vera. You're up early."

"Yep yep," Vera responded from the bedroom door with her usual wide grin. "I'm always excited to help out, y' know? Plus, we need to get there early. There are only 3 parking spaces."

"Oh, right. Wouldn't want to... not park, I guess. I'll be down in a sec."

"Okayyyy."

Jeez.

An hour later, Vera and Kara were cruising down the streets out of the gated area they lived in and into the city. The futuristic streetlights were on, and one or two people were jogging along the road in weird luminescent jackets.

Probably so they don't get turned into roadkill.

As they neared City Hall, Vera took a left down the road and came to a stop in front of a single-story building. It was made of the same material that all the buildings seemed to be made of, but it was clear that this one needed some work.

As if Vera could read her thoughts, she offered an explanation.

"The federal funding to this area is muddled up in some local government scheme to embezzle public funds. Everybody knows about it, but there hasn't been any action against those in charge yet. So in light of that, it makes more sense to feed those that need it in a rundown shack than it does to starve them in a beautiful building."

"That makes sense."

Kara got down and looked closer at the building. It seemed to be empty and locked up.

"Vera, there's no one here. We're too early."

"Oh, right. I come here so early that the custodian gave me my own key. So I can come open up for the day whenever. Neat, isn't it?"

"Yeah. Neat."

"You don't have to help out if you don't want to, Nana. I realize it's not for everyone. I just want to spend this time with you, that's all."

The sincerity in her voice was disarming. It twisted the knife that had pierced Kara's heart the night before, and she knew she couldn't leave things as they were.

"Hey, now. I never said I wasn't going to help. I'm excited to be here as well."

The telltale smile flashed back into place, and Kara breathed a sigh of relief.

I just have to suffer through this one time, anyway. It's going to be okay. How much work could charity be?

*****

Kara had never realized just how much work charity could be until now.

Every single bone in her body objected as she carried around piles of plates, large platters of food, and multiple packs of water. There seemed to be no end to those that needed serving.

"We need more forks on Line 3!"

Kara sped off at once, making a beeline straight for the forks. As she threaded her way between the tables and queues in the soup kitchen, she thought back to mere hours ago and her reluctance to participate.

Boy, was I being stupid.

Despite her self-assertion to the contrary, Kara had fully expected the exercise to be uncomfortable, challenging, and tasking on her body. And she'd been entirely right. She had started out serving, but knew nothing about portions and kept messing up. The supervisor had politely asked her to let him have a turn, but the few minutes she'd been upfront had shown her something she hadn't been counting on; the heart-warming goodness of a grateful smile. As she handed out food to those in need, she could see the happiness blossom in their eyes. It tugged at her heartstrings in a way that she hadn't expected. She had sat idle for a few minutes, just basking in the feeling for the first time. And then the call had gone up.

"Someone with free hands, please get me another stack of bread rolls!"

Kara looked up to see who would go, but almost immediately realized that no one was free. And then she realized that she was free. She could still help.

She turned to Vera, who was in the middle of ladling out some punch.

"Dear, where are the bread rolls?"

Now, hours later, Kara had not only run supply for every other volunteer at the place solo, so much so that she knew where everything was and how much was left, she'd also managed to make the entire crowd that much more cheerful. Everyone was friendly and wanted to chat, and she found herself enjoying the fellowship of the soup kitchen more than she'd enjoyed anything since she'd found herself in this body.

A quick scan told her that they were done for the day, and she could relax. So after passing off the forks, she dropped into her seat, exhausted through and through.

God, I've never been so happy to have taken my meds and supplements. That was a huge workout.

But despite the aches, Kara was strangely happy. And her smile, a genuine smile like she hadn't had on in ages, stayed on even as Vera's car pulled up to another building.

"Where are we now? Is there another charity event here?"

"No, no. You've done way more than you should've already, Nana. You were amazing!"

"Well, it was to help others, right? Had to do my very best."

Vera broke out into a grin and gave Kara an endearing side hug through her seatbelt.

"This is Jeff's office. I need to go pick some stuff up from my school's walk-in office. I'm gonna apply for a scholarship pretty soon, so I need to start getting things ready, y' know? I'd love for you to come with, but since the whole 2020 incident, there have been some stringent rules about who can go in and out of a school office. So you'll stay here, and then we'll all go home together. He took next week off work and just needed to get some stuff from his office first."

"Okay. Will you be very long?"

"Not at all. The school office is a block down, and long queues aren't allowed. I'll be back in less than a half-hour."

Kara got down from the car and waved Vera away, insisting she could go on her own. As she approached the large white doors of the single-story office building, her mind unearthed a topic she'd been meaning to broach with Jeff for a while now…

*****

"I still can't believe you'd make your office a replica of the house! What happened to a change of environment, huh?"

"Come on, Nana! I like it this way! You're hurting my feelings!"

Kara and Jeff shared a small laugh at the dialogue. Jeff had decided to pass the time with Kara by showing her around his office, which she'd never been to. To her surprise and mock dismay, she found that he had asked the decorator to make it precisely the same interior as the house.

As their laughter died down, Kara decided to make her move.

"Jeff, I need to ask you something."

"Shoot, Nana."

Kara took a moment to think out how to phrase what she was about to say.

"Okay. So, Vera is a nice kid. Probably the best teenager I've ever met in my life. But she's not... really your sister. But you treat her like it. You address her as such, shower her with presents, show up for her virtual PTA meetings, calm her down when she's fidgety, and discipline her when she leaves her music playing too loud. You even took me in when she asked you to. Why?"

Jeff seemed to be taken aback by the question. His expression soon recovered, however. He considered it for a bit, then gave his reply.

"Why, because she's family. I'd do anything for family. Anyone would."

"I understand that. Anyone would. But she's not really your family. We're not related to you by blood. So-"

"So what?" he asserted, in a firm but soft voice.

"Huh?"

"I mean it. So what? So what if Vera was adopted? So what if you were estranged from us till now? So what if we don't have blood ties? None of that matters."

"But it does. That's what family is, after all."

"No, Nana. That's not it. Family isn't just the people you're born to or the people you happen to share blood with. Family is more than that. Family is the people that choose to be a part of your life. To share the day to day worries and humor with you. Family is choosing to sacrifice for someone else, choosing to love someone else. It's thinking about them before yourself. Family is as simple as the people we call family. And so, Vera is my sister, because we chose to be family. And you're my Nana because we choose to be family. Or at least, I hope you'd choose me. I did ask, after all."

Jeff laughed off the last bit as a spot of humor, but Kara remembered it clearly.

"I'm Jeff, Vera's brother. And your new grandson, if you'll let me. "

"Nice to meet you, Jeff. I'm Kara."

"Can I call you Nana?"

"Umm… sure. If you want to."

"Splendid!"

She'd thought nothing of it then, but thinking back on it, he'd been deadly serious. He had truly treated her like a grandson would. Even without a blood relationship, even before he knew what she was like, he'd chosen to make her comfortable and loved.

And Kara had loved every moment of it.

"I love you, Nana. And Vera does, too."

It was as if he'd heard her thoughts. Tears came to Kara's eyes as she realized all of a sudden what type of person she'd been all along.

"Don't cry, Nana. It's all good, y' know?"

"You don't understand. There's-"

Kara's statement was cut short by a searing pain through her chest. She clutched at it and struggled to breathe normally. It felt like some large malevolent force was pressing down on her torso, choking her and crushing her heart as it did so.

"Nana! What's wrong?"

Kara couldn't respond. Her consciousness began to slip, and she fell to the floor as her vision faded and faded and faded…

*****

-bad physical condition, can't be un-

Kara regained consciousness with a start, her eyes snapping open like a turtle trap. The rest of her, however, wasn't so readily mobile. She couldn't seem to move her hands or legs properly.

She looked around and saw doctors through blurred vision and couldn't seem to control herself.

"W-where am I?"

There was no immediate answer, as other people seemed to be moving furiously through the room. Or maybe that was an illusion. Her vision refused to focus correctly, and the movement around her seemed to all blur into one convoluted image.

Focus, Kara. Focus.

"Nana?"

It was Vera's voice. The distress in it was apparent, and it hurt Kara deeply. Or maybe that was just the heart condition.

"Nana, can you hear me?"

"Yea, Vera. I can hear you. What's happening to me?"

"Your heart… it's giving way."

"Oh."

Sniffling, Vera came closer so Kara could see her.

"It's not fair that you came into our lives just to have to leave again. We won't be able to take care of you at the house like this. We'll come visit you every day, but it won't be the same thing."

"I- I'm not sure I'm going to be around very long anymore, dear. I think- I think I'm dying."

The sniffles intensified until Vera was sobbing softly onto Kara's arm. The warm tears ran down her skin and made her feel better and worse at the same time. She was conflicted.

A firm hand grasped her palm on her other side.

"Jeff?"

"Yes, Nana. I'm here. I'm here."

He was trying to sound more put together than he felt, but it wasn't working out so well.

"I have a confession to make. I don't think I'm gonna make it, and I can't go out knowing I didn't come clean. Vera, Jeff, I'm not-"

"Really our grandmother?" Jeff finished for her.

"Huh? Ah, right. Jacqui must have told you now, I'm sure."

"Actually, Nana, she told us the day after you moved in with us. As soon as she found out you were gone."

This news confused Kara intensely.

"Huh? So why-?"

"I told you already, Nana. Family isn't just who you're born to or who's blood you share. It's a choice. You chose to come with Vera because you two had a connection. You didn't know whether we were rich or comfortable or not. But you felt it, and you came. You chose to make us your family, and we accepted you. By the time Jacqui told us, we didn't really care, y' know? You're our Nana through and through. And we love you."

The tears that had escaped her eyes in the office earlier flowed freely now, and the three sobbed together for a time.

After a while, a stern voice insisted that Jeff and Vera had to take a break and eat something, or they'd be forced off the premises. They grudgingly obeyed, each one giving Kara a light squeeze before letting go.

"This is a really touching farewell, Kara."

The voice was one she'd heard before. Despite being unable to see her, Kara responded, her voice weakening by the minute.

"Hello, Gelisa."

"It's a shame, you know. You were my first friend here that had all her marbles intact. Well, for the most part, I guess. Only a crazy person would pull that stunt that you did with Vera over there. But I like a little crazy too."

Kara found herself laughing, despite not having nearly enough energy for it.

"Yeah, well. Laugh it up. You're going to leave here pretty soon and go somewhere better. But I'm back to square one now."

"Sorry about that, Gelisa. I swear I'm not doing this on purpose."

That line brought a smile to Gelisa's face, and Kara heard her say something under her breath. It sounded like a prayer.

"I just wish we had some more time together. Maybe in another life, we could've been best friends in high school."

"That would've been great. If only we could turn the clock back on life as we knew it, eh?"

"Don't believe in reincarnation, then?"

"I don't know, Gelisa. Maybe?"

"That settles it then. If you're ever reincarnated into the world, let me be your friend again, alright? Promise?"

"Yeah. I promise."

*****

A half-hour later, Vera reentered the private visiting room. She'd brisk walked all the way back from the mess and seemed to have eaten even less than Kara herself had since the incident. Not too long after, Jeff returned as well, his cheeks looking better but having a painful, sallow look to them.

They stayed there with her for an hour, and then another. In silence, enjoying what they knew were their last moments with her now. They'd tried to tell her otherwise, but she was irreparably dying. Her heart had run its course, vessels and all.

Suddenly, the sharp pain resumed, and Kara knew that her time was up. She fought through the pain, stretching her arms out to touch both Jeff and Vera. She squeezed them both tight, and they came in for one last hug.

"I think it's time for me to go now."

"Nana, don't-"

"It's okay. It's fine. I'm old. This is perfectly natural. There was no way I was going to survive that heart failure anyway. But I'm in way less pain than I thought I would be in, and that's something to be glad about, right?"

Vera nodded, but tears streaked down her face as she did so. She tightened her grip on Kara's hand as the old woman's eyes slowly faded, and her consciousness followed suit.

"We'll miss you, Nana."

"I'll miss you both, too."

"-miss you, Kara."

We'll miss you, Kara.

I'll miss you too.

*****

CHAPTER 7
Conclusion

"Kara? Kara!"

Mom?

"Dale! I think she's finally coming to! Come quick!"

Mother? Dale?

"Thank goodness. I couldn't have taken any more of this."

Kara's cognitive functions were taking a while to return to 100%, but she was sure that she'd heard her mother and Dale. Her entire body seemed to have been asleep for ages, and everything was moving sluggishly. But it wasn't her usual age-related crawling. This was different, like Sunday evenings after eating way too much.

As her eyes fluttered open, she found herself looking at a ceiling. Shafts of bright sunlight light fell across it in thin shafts. It was a very pale pink, sort of like someone had wanted her room to be a hot pink box, but her mother insisted the ceilings be normal, and so they'd met in the middle.

I'm in my own room now.

It was warm, just like she had left it, with the same familiar softness beneath her.

"Mom?"

Her throat hurt from the effort, but it was an almost forgotten type of pain. It was temporary, triggered by something she did.

"Yes, Kara?"

The voice that responded was on the verge of tears. Kara recognized it as her mom's happy voice. She struggled up to rest on her elbows, and then looked around.

Her mother was seated at her side, tears flowing down her face. She was looking at Kara with disbelief and relief in her eyes, both struggling one over the other to hold her tongue. She tried to speak again, but couldn't.

"Your mother is a bit overwhelmed, Kara. So am I, to be perfectly honest about it. We're so glad to have you back."

Turning towards the door of her room, she saw Dale standing in the door frame. He looked relieved as well, and from the stubble on his chin, Kara could tell that they'd both been as worried as they said. If not more.

Kara was about to respond to Dale when something in the back of her mind spoke up.

What is a real family?

Kara had been through a lot, and she had gotten the feeling that she'd been irreparably changed by her experiences in a positive light. And this was one of them. After her talk with Jeff, she'd immediately begun to reflect on how her actions and attitudes towards people in general- and especially towards Dale, could be the cause of her misery and unhappiness. But she was willing to bet it wasn't too late for some changes.

"Thanks, Dad. I have no idea what really happened, but I'm sure you'll fill me in when I'm better"

There was a stunned silence following this statement as both parents were taken aback by what they'd just heard.

"Honey, did you just-"

"You called me your-?"

Kara rolled her eyes, not in her usual exasperated way, but in a more comedic way.

"Yes, I did. I've been through a lot the past few weeks, but it taught me a few lessons that I think I needed to experience firsthand. And one of them was about family. I can't be hung up about my dad forever. I can't resist change that makes others happy *just because.* I appreciate what you do for my mom, and for me. You chose to treat us like family, and you deserve the same in return."

The two adults stared at her, dumbfounded even more so than before.

"Well, thank you," Dale said, finally breaking the silence. "Well, since you bring up family, we have some news that we've been a bit too distraught to really celebrate. Emma?"

Kara's mom had finally gathered her wits about her and took a deep breath before speaking.

"We're expecting," she said rather shortly. "You're gonna have a sister. Or a brother. Either or."

Kara stared at them both with wide eyes, their news somehow superseding all she had just been through in importance.

"We just found out ourselves a few days ago, when we came to get you from the hospital. We couldn't properly celebrate until now, though."

"That's great! I'm gonna be a big sister!"

Kara sprung forward from the bed, her weariness gone. She grabbed her mother and hugged her tight, easing slightly when she heard her moan in protest. As they sat there together, Dale came over and draped his arms around them both.

"Hope you don't mind if I butt in?"

"No. We're a family, after all."

*****

"-and so, when we got the call that you'd been involved in an accident, we had no idea you'd be in a 2-month coma. But a few days ago, your brain activity started to pick up, and we were allowed to bring you home and care of you ourselves. And then two days ago, you woke up with no complications."

"2 months? Wow. That's forever. Wait. Does that mean I'm not grounded anymore?" Kara asked with a mischievous grin.

"Actually when we heard the news, your mom swore we'd go easy on you if you'd just come back to us. So I guess you *do* get to go scot-free."

"Well, I'm not gonna say no to having a phone again. But I promise I've learned my lesson."

"We hope so. Certainly seems like it."

"Trust me, I've learned a lot more than you could imagine."

Dale laughed heartily as his wife clicked her tongue the way she did when she was impatient. He decided to let her out of the bear hug she'd been in the entire time he'd been speaking.

Kara said goodbye to her parents and stepped out of the house and into the cold morning air. She had a lot of places to go to, charities to sign up for, and a girl to go befriend.

She was about to be a whole different person. Again.

www.ingramcontent.com/pod-product-compliance
Lightning Source LLC
Chambersburg PA
CBHW050953050726

47592CB00007B/2554